MONASTERY NIGHTMARE

ROSS H. SPENCER

THE MYSTERIOUS PRESS • New York

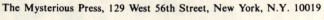

Copyright © 1986 by Ross H. Spencer
All rights reserved.
The Mysterious Press, 129 West 56th Street, New York, N.Y. 10019

Printed in the United States of America
First Printing: March 1986
10 9 8 7 6 5 4 3 2 1

Library of Congress Cataloging-in-Publication Data

Spencer, Ross H.
    Monastery nightmare.

    I. Title.
PS3569.P454M6   1986   813′.54   85-43164
ISBN 0-89296-233-X

MONASTERY NIGHTMARE

OTHER BOOKS BY ROSS H. SPENCER

The Dada Caper
The Reggis Arms Caper
The Stranger City Caper
The Abu Wahab Caper
The Radish River Caper
Echoes of Zero
The Missing Bishop

MONASTERY NIGHTMARE is dedicated to Zeke Paulishen, Red Amadio, Paul Amadio, Tut Javorsky, Fred Gioglio, and Nick LaVolpa, with whom I had the privilege of serving during the last war this country's politicians permitted us to win . . . And to Shirley Spencer, who has served with me through thick and thin . . . and thin . . . and thin. . . .

. . . success is just another bass drum . . . big, loud, expensive . . . and hollow . . .

Monroe D. Underwood

MONASTERY NIGHTMARE

At the west end of a long hallway on the third floor of the old Peerless Building on Chicago's West Adams Street there was a small room, the frosted glass of its door stenciled LASSITER PRIVATE INVESTIGATIONS, *its interior dusty and dim, its venetian blind arrayed in tight defense against the onslaughts of the July sun. On a wall, facing a desk, there was a mirror, broken in three places and taped together. The desk had known better days. It listed noticeably to starboard on spindly, spavined legs, struggling valiantly to support a telephone and a telephone-answering device, a morning newspaper, a crumpled half-pack of Marlboro cigarettes, an empty Walgreen's coffee carton, a wrapper from a pecan roll, a nearly depleted bottle of aspirin tablets, a Zippo lighter, a chipped glass ashtray spilling over with cigarette butts, and a yellow legal pad on which had been scribbled a multitude of notations.*

In a corner of the room there was a green filing cabinet and beside it stood a small, badly chipped refrigerator repainted a streaky flat black. There was a sagging brown leatherette couch with a torn cushion. There were two wooden chairs in the room, one to the immediate left of the desk, the other, of the swivel variety, behind the desk. The first chair was vacant but the swivel chair was occupied by a heavy-shouldered man of some forty years. The man's name was Luke Lassiter.

Lassiter was developing a slight paunch and his receding, dark, wavy hair was graying slightly at the temples. A crooked white scar ambled aimlessly down his left cheek, a reminder of a broken beer bottle brawl in a tavern at 18th and State, not the shrapnel wound he so often represented it to be. His eyes were wide-set, hound-dog brown, bloodshot and tired. His nose had been broken and improperly set. His mouth was thin-lipped, tight, and turned down at the corners. His stubborn jaw was in

ROSS H. SPENCER

need of a shave, his shirt collar was undone and there was a faint streak of mustard on his necktie. He wore a Green Beret pin on a lapel of his wrinkled, sweat-stained plaid sports jacket. He was suffering from a monumental hangover, the result of drinking vast quantities of Stroh's beer with a man named Stash Dubinski at Bessie Barnum's Circus Tap on 72nd Court across the street from the big Leffingwell Historical Museum in Elmwood Park. Hangover or no hangover, Lassiter worked diligently at the yellow legal pad on his desk, writing a line, reading it, crossing out a word or two, repeating the process over and over again until the paper looked like a map of Hiroshima after the bomb. This was a practice of long standing with Lassiter, who was a warrior on two fronts and taking a thorough whipping on both. He was a second-rate private detective and a third-rate writer of fiction, hacking away at his yellow legal pad while waiting for his telephone to ring. The phone rang occasionally, just often enough to keep him off the relief rolls, and over the years it had dispatched him into a lot of Chicago dark corners where he'd won a few, lost a few and settled for a few draws. But once, long ago, Lassiter had sold a short story, something called "Lilacs Are Fatal." He'd never scored again and he'd stopped submitting his work to the agent responsible for his single sale but he'd patiently awaited the arrival of the idea for a blockbusting novel and in his wake he'd left a great many auspicious beginnings that faltered and fell by the wayside, usually within fewer than one hundred pages. He was a loser in the time-honored tradition of Chicago losers, trapped on a treadmill to nowhere, and he knew that he'd be willing to pay a great price to write a book that would attract national attention.

Then the fates got wind of Lassiter's ambition and at a seminar or convention or wherever the fates assemble they arranged for Lassiter to write his book. On his own terms.

At a great price.

1

The telephone jingled and I pounced on it like a skinny cat pounces on a fat canary. Hangover or no hangover, one should never underestimate the reflexes of a Chicago private detective two months in arrears on his office rent.

Instinctively I went into Routine #1. I rustled the sports section of the *Chicago Tribune*, mumbled a few words to an imaginary client, something about being glad that you're so pleased with my handling of the matter, Mr. Bumbleflutz, opened a desk drawer, kicked it shut with a bang, and barked, "Lassiter Private Investigations!" into the mouthpiece. Wasted theatrics. The caller was a Latino who wanted Acme Body and Fender Repair. I growled a four-letter word and returned my attention to the legal pad and a daring jewel heist aboard a Jamaica-bound luxury liner caught in a hurricane. The phone rang again and I went into Routine #2. Routine #2 consisted of letting the damn thing ring five or six times. When a man's terribly busy there will be times when he simply can't get to the phone in a hurry.

The voice on the other end was hoarse. It reminded me of a dull can-opener working on a rusty sardine tin but it was authoritative, a voice accustomed to dishing out orders and having them obeyed without question. It said, "This Lassiter? Doan wanna talk with nobody else no-how. Gotta be Lassiter hisself."

I dug my Zippo from under the pecan roll wrapper and got a cigarette going. I said, "This is Lassiter hisself."

The voice said, "Wall, Lassiter, y'all speakin' to Reverend

3

Johnny Huskin." He waited for that to sink in. It did. I was wide awake now.

I said, "Yes, Reverend Huskin, may I be of assistance?"

"Reckon y'all might. Wanna see y'all up here in my offices in th' Randolph Buildin' come three o'clock this here afternoon."

If my information was accurate, Reverend Johnny Huskin was a good old down-home boy, Tennessee or Louisiana, and he had the grits-and-greens drawl to prove it. I said, "Huh-uh, Reverend, can't make it quite that soon." This one would require some thought. Fools rush in and come out on stretchers.

Heat flared in Huskin's hoarseness. He said, "Now, looky here, Lassiter, this here might be important. Y'all in business or *not?*"

I said, "I'll know more by the end of the month."

It went over Huskin's head. He said, "Wall, these here yaller pages puts y'all a lot closer'n any these here other detective agencies. Y'all must be able to spare *some*body."

"I work alone, Reverend."

"Awright, when *kin* y'all make it up thisaway?"

"What's the difficulty?"

"I ain't even sure I got one. Thass where y'all come in."

"Can't you be just a bit more specific?"

"Wall, less us juss say that there's a li'l ole personal matter I want looked into."

That was a bit better. I said, "Hold it a minute, Reverend. Let me check my appointments."

Huskin pressed. He said, "So how's lak mebbe three-fahty-fav?"

I kicked it around. What the hell, nothing ventured, nothing gained. My father's very words just before he'd climbed the ladder to repair the chimney. He'd come down a lot faster than he'd gone up and, when they loaded him into the ambulance, he'd said, "Well, son, I took a shot at it." Taking a shot at it was a Lassiter family tradition and I am very big on Lassiter family traditions. I said, "All right, Reverend, I'll take a shot at it."

Then I hung up and mopped sweat from my forehead with my wrinkled blue bandana.

2

I knew a great deal about Reverend Johnny Huskin. He'd crossed the Mason-Dixon Line with an out-of-tune piano, an utterly atrocious voice and a heartfelt way with a gospel song. He'd sung those old melodies the way they were meant to be sung, the way they'd been sung in the brush-arbor churches of Appalachia back in the days when the wearing of lipstick branded a woman an out-and-out harlot. He'd sold recordings, hundreds of thousands of them, and he'd preached a mercilessly uncompromising religious doctrine, country-style.

The country-style evangelist is a horse of another color. He doesn't advise you, nor does he reason with you. He *attacks* you. He grabs you by the collar, jerks you into the woodshed and tans your hide. You don't go to sleep under the preaching of an honest-to-God country evangelist and Johnny Huskin was probably the best in the business, ignoring lecterns to storm across auditorium stages brandishing a tattered old Bible, leaping around like a demented kangaroo, kicking things, romping, stomping, dusting the carpet in the process, lighting full-tilt into television, moving pictures, girly magazines, plunging necklines, short skirts and wishy-washy religions. He raved about Hades fire and brimstone and how y'all better git squared away with God, brother, on account of y'all juss ain't gonna lak it in Hayull, *rilly!* He could weep at the drop of a hat, his vivid descriptions of the end of the world would have kept a New Guinea headhunter awake all night and his altar-calls would have melted the hearts of Geronimo and every Apache in Arizona. Johnny Huskin peddled Bibles, sheet music, bumper

ROSS H. SPENCER

stickers, posters, pennants, badges, photographs of Johnny Huskin and trips to the Holy Land. He didn't drink, he didn't smoke, he didn't gamble and he took an extremely dim view of sex. He buried his take in the vaults of the Chicago Second National Bank under the snow-white banner of the Johnny Huskin Evangelistic Association. He sweetened the most modest of salaries with an unlimited expense account and he lived like a feudal baron in a sprawling fourteen-room stone mansion on eight wooded acres in White Birch Knolls, an exquisite little village located a few miles northwest of Chicago. His only hobby was a firearms collection that would have turned the Detroit Purple Gang green with envy. I'd never met Johnny Huskin but I'd seen a few of his telecasts and I had him pegged as a charlatan. But I'm a cynic. Private detectives usually are.

I sat at my rickety desk, smoking, frowning and thinking. If this was happenstance it was a red-letter case but truth is stranger than fiction. I'd just have to see how the cards fell.

I picked up the phone, started to dial, thought better of it and hung up. It was two o'clock by the battery-powered clock on my north wall when I thumbed through a cumbersome stack of bills, shrugged, shoved the entire bundle into my wastebasket, switched on my telephone-answering device and headed down the two flights of stairs to the lobby. Taking the stairs was necessary. The Peerless Building elevator was out of order.

3

In the Peerless Building lobby Lieutenant Jake Perry was standing at the magazine counter, paging through the *Chicago Sun-Times*. Jake was a Chicago Homicide detective, a tall, lean, leathery guy, sharp hazel-eyed, hard-nosed, a decent cop by anybody's standards. He glanced up, grinned, pointed a pistol-style finger at me and wiggled his thumb. He said, "Bang, you're dead."

I said, "You're only half right." Jake mooched a cigarette. We went back a long way, Jake Perry and I. When my family had moved to Chicago from Hubbard, Ohio, we'd lived in the Perry family's Logan Square apartment building and Jake and I had been high school classmates. We'd played football together and we'd learned to drink together. Jake had gone into the Air Force and I'd joined the Army to qualify for the Green Berets. Then it had been the Chicago Police Academy for Jake and the Merchant Marine for me. When I'd ditched the seaman's life, Jake had talked me into joining the police force but three years of that had been plenty. I'd figured that if a man was determined to starve to death he could do it on his own and I'd been proving it ever since. I said, "Working, Jake?"

He shook his head. "Not now. I'm doing the graveyard grind with Barry Nash. You know Nash?"

"Fat-assed guy?"

"Used to be. On a diet now."

"Yeah, I know him. Care for a beer?"

"No time. Meeting Helen for lunch. She's shopping."

"You may have a week."

7

ROSS H. SPENCER

"Gonna be in the Sherwood?"

"For a while."

"I like that little barmaid."

"Mary O'Rourke? So do I."

"Just saw Kenny Blossom leaving the Sherwood."

"That's okay, just so he was *leaving*."

"Cheap sonofabitch. George Halas must have trained him."
Like most Chicago football fans, Jake Perry despised George
Halas. I whistled a line of "Bear Down, Chicago Bears" and
waved so long.

We were in a hot July of what was rapidly developing into a
typical Chicago summer. The Cubs were in last place, so were
the White Sox, the Bears had dismissed one bargain-basement
coach and hired another, the city was averaging four murders a
day and half of these were police officers, mugging and rape
stats were on the upswing, the fire department was threatening
to go on strike and there was a riot in Humboldt Park every
Sunday.

The afternoon was sultry and the sky was cloudless blue. I
waved to old Nick Spanzetti, the corner newsstand proprietor,
and he waved back. He hollered, "No score, middle of the
second, Luke!" Nick was a baseball maniac and the Cubs were
finishing up a three-game set with St. Louis at Clark and Addison. The Sherwood Forest Pub was located in the basement of
the Peerless Building. It was a dim, cool cavernous establishment
with heavy, rough-hewn beams supported by eight-by-eight
uprights rounded and disguised as trees from which protruded a
great many black-feathered arrows. The splintered walls of the
place were adorned by deer antlers, long bows, copper ale mugs,
tarnished hunting horns and several fake-parchment posters
announcing a reward of £100 for information leading to the
arrest of the outlaw Robin Hood, formerly known as Robert of
Locksley. Something about killing the King's deer. "Green-
sleeves" or "Scarborough Fair" would have blended nicely with
the decor but the brown plastic radio on the backbar was
playing "When My Blue Moon Turns to Gold Again." Mary
O'Rourke was a country music buff.

She stood behind the deserted bar, clad in a feathered green
cap, gauzy green blouse, loose leather vest, tight brown suede

8

MONASTERY NIGHTMARE

shorts and long green stockings, the prescribed attire for all Sherwood Forest girls, and she filled the costume to perfection. She smiled her fetching, lopsided, white-toothed smile and said, "Mucho Macho just checked out."

"Blossom? Yeah, Jake Perry told me. Glad I missed him."

"Didn't stay long. Nobody bought him a drink. How're you betting the ball game, Luke?" She had a bright, chipper voice.

I straddled a bar stool and pointed to the Stroh's tap. I said, "There's a couple of things I never bet on. Baseball's one of them."

"I'll bite. What's the other?"

"Women."

"Hang in there, you gotta get lucky sometime."

"Maybe on baseball."

Mary O'Rourke was a pert, pretty, thirtyish Irish lass with short, dark hair and long-lashed, sparkling, smoky-blue eyes. She'd proposed to me once. In fact she'd proposed to me four or five times. Her most recent had been couched in logic. She'd said, "What the hell, we work in the same building, don't we?"

I'd said, "So?"

She'd said, "We could drive to work together. Think of the money we'd save."

I'd said, "You'll have to do better than that."

She'd winked at me, a slow, naughty wink. "Come on, Luke, there's more and you know it." There was more, all right. Mary O'Rourke was a Class AAA scorcher in bed. Her only drawback was that she didn't know when to roll over and call it a night. On more than one occasion I'd left her near-northside apartment with my knees buckling. I liked her company. She had the Irish sense of humor, she was genuine, she did things with gusto and she could cook. She brought my Stroh's and I downed it thirstily. She said, "Anything happening?"

I shrugged. "Three-forty-five appointment in the Randolph Building."

"Concerning?"

"He didn't get into it."

Mary nodded approvingly. "Glad it's a 'he.' " She popped for a beer, a custom when the manager wasn't around. She said, "When are you coming up to see my new etchings?"

9

ROSS H. SPENCER

I said, "The very damn minute I recover from seeing your old etchings."

Mary giggled. It was a pleasant, lilting sound, a laugh that a man could live with. "Was it really that rough?"

"Baby, you know it!"

"Well, gee whiz, Luke, I just do what comes naturally."

"I know that. Same holds true for mountain lions."

"Sure, but I don't scratch."

"The hell you don't scratch."

"Oh, maybe just a little but not real hard."

I snorted. I said, "How'd you like to look at my shoulders?"

Mary put her hands on her hips. She licked her lips provocatively and there was that slow wink again. She said, "That'd be okay for starters."

The little backbar radio was playing "Your Cheating Heart" and it was almost three-thirty before I knew it.

4

I made my way through the graying canyons of the late-afternoon Loop, through the din of horns and traffic whistles and snarling engines and squealing brakes, through carbon monoxide fumes and odors from fast food joints, through legions of fat women carrying parcels and dragging screaming, chocolate-smeared children. I spotted a pay telephone, headed for it, then swerved back into the northbound current of humanity. Why take damn fool chances?

The spacious ground floor of the recently remodeled Randolph Building was done in black marble or an excellent imitation thereof. It was studded with swank little gift shops that featured candles, crystal vases, flowers, imported tobaccos, costume jewelry, perfumes and old clocks, all ridiculously overpriced. I stopped to check the building register and found the Johnny Huskin Evangelistic Association listed as being located on the fourth floor.

All of the fourth floor, as it turned out. I stepped from the swift, smooth-riding elevator into a hushed lobby and the overpowering scent of roses. There were roses everywhere, roses on tables, on bookcases, in wall niches, on the floor, roses by the vase, by the basket and by the bowl. Red roses—no whites, no pinks, no yellows. From somewhere faint tape-recorded chimes played "Sweet Hour of Prayer." There was something downright funereal about the entire layout and I found myself looking around for a coffin. Seeing none, I settled for a huge, white-thatched woman in a high-collared black dress. With her mane of snowy hair she reminded me a great deal of Mt.

Everest. She wore wire-framed spectacles, a scowl to withstand the ages and a big yellow and blue badge that read I'M SO GLAD MY JESUS LIFTED ME. Considering her bulk it must have been one helluva job, even for Him. She sat at a low, white Formica-topped counter behind a veritable jungle of red roses, operating a console that might have been pirated from a spaceliner headed for Ludos IV, wherever that is. After a very long time she turned ponderously to glare at me over the wire frames of her glasses. She said, "Your business, sir?"

I said, "Well, I used to be in the Merchant Marine but now I'm into private investigations."

She sniffed, drew back and pursed her lips disapprovingly. She looked at me as though I'd just crawled from under a flat, mossy rock. She said, "Young man, are you inebriated?"

I glanced around the room at the sea of red roses. I said, "Jesus Christ, I hope so."

She responded to a flashing blue light on her console, punched a button and said, "Praise the Lord, Johnny Huskin Evangelistic Association . . . Yes, ma'am, contributions are accepted at this address . . ." Then she riveted a rigid, frigid gaze to the mustard streak on my necktie and said, "Sir, I am very busy. Your name and the purpose of your visit, *please*."

"Luke Lassiter. I got a three-fahty-fav appointment with the Rev."

She flipped a nasty-looking red key on the console and spoke briefly in subdued tones. She gave me a chilling look and said, "Reverend Huskin will see you now." She motioned to her right, a grandiose gesture, like a Cossack general in a Grade B movie. She said, "Down the hall, please. First door to your left."

I stumbled over a gilded coal bucket full of red roses, grabbed the countertop for support and overturned a ceramic urn of roses into Mt. Everest's lap. I gave her a ghastly smile and said, "Oops!"

It was the least I could do.

5

I located Reverend Johnny Huskin in a large, beige-carpeted room, the pecan-paneled walls of which were covered by dozens of photographs of the mighty man in action. I saw Johnny Huskin counseling repentant sinners at altars, I saw Johnny Huskin raising his arms beseechingly heavenward, Johnny Huskin shaking his fist at the Devil, Johnny Huskin studying his Bible, Johnny Huskin sitting on a hollow log communing with nature, Johnny Huskin kneeling in silent prayer, Johnny Huskin preaching up a storm, Johnny Huskin smiling, Johnny Huskin weeping over the transgressions of this sin-soaked world, Johnny Huskin doing all the things that make great evangelists great.

In a distant corner of the room there was a white-and-gold baby grand piano and on it was a white leather-bound Bible the size of a Mafia wedding cake. On a table were scattered several copies of a slim, brightly colored book entitled *The Sawdust Trail to Glory. The Sawdust Trail to Glory* had been written by Reverend Johnny Huskin. Reverend Johnny Huskin was "The Modern-Day Billy Sunday" according to the dust jacket. The book had been published by the Johnny Huskin Evangelistic Association Press. About 150 pages: $27.95.

Huskin sat in a high-backed, black Corinthian leather chair behind a paper-cluttered desk big enough to host a Big Ten Conference track-and-field meet. He was a shade older and a few pounds slimmer than he appeared during his Sunday morning telecasts but he was an impressive, clean-shaven, granite-jawed man of perhaps fifty, sandy-haired, bright blue-eyed, hawk-faced, broad-shouldered, barrel-chested, wearing a tailor-made medium-blue double-breasted suit, white shirt and slim black necktie, its white silk-embroidered *JH* corralled by a beautiful circular pin composed of tiny golden crosses. There was a red rose in the buttonhole of his left lapel. He studied me for a long moment before saying, "Siddown, Lassiter." I complied and Huskin closed a bulky gray plastic folder and leaned back in his big black chair. He placed his fingertips carefully together. His nails had been nicely done and they shone in the soft bluish glow of his brass fluorescent desk lamp. Johnny Huskin had come a long way from the barnyard. He cleared his throat raspingly and said, "Awright, Lassiter, less us git right at it. What y'all chargin' fer a evenin's work?"

I said, "The going rate. Hundred and a half plus expenses."

Huskin's bright blue eyes glinted. He said, "Hunnert an' a half comes on reasonable enough but y'all gonna have to skip that there expenses clause on account of there ain't gonna be no expenses 'ceptin' mebbe a li'l ole bit of gasoline."

I shrugged. You can dicker with a mountaineer but a dirt farmer is another matter. A farmer will beat you out of something if it's no more than a chaw of Mail Pouch. Under normal conditions I'd have told him to go scratch his ass but these conditions weren't normal. For me they never were. I wouldn't have recognized normal conditions if they'd walked up and seized me by the testicles.

Huskin took a deep breath, like he did on television before coming down hard on expensive whiskey and cheap women. He said, "Now, Lassiter, I 'spect y'all kin unnerstan' how a feller in my position ain't particular anxious to git mixed up in no scandal what with me carryin' on th' work of Th' Lord an' ever'thin'." When I didn't say anything Huskin continued. "Why, they's a whole passel of fokes out there juss dyin' to see th' House of Th' Lord come a-tumblin' down. They's sittin' aroun' taverns an' sportin' houses waitin' to pick fault with Th' Master's earthly servants so's they kin rare back an' laugh an' say, 'See there? I tole you so! I done knowed it all th' time!' "

I nodded and hoped to Christ he wasn't leading up to what I was afraid he might be leading up to. Huskin brushed a bit of lint from his cuff and said, "Lassiter, I ain't ezzackly nowheres near positive but I think mebbe I got me whatchacall a slight

MONASTERY NIGHTMARE

domestic problem. Y'all knows what I mean when I says 'slight domestic problem'?"

I said, "Probably, but I'd rather you spelled it out."

"I'm about to do that. There is times when I gits me a notion that my wife's weekly wimmen's writers club meetin's amounts to considerable more than weekly wimmen's writers club meetin's. Y'all with me, Lassiter?"

"I think so. Is your wife a writer?"

Huskin said, "Shoot, my wife never wrote nothin' more interestin' than a grocery list but sometimes she reads this here gothic garbage which is writ by fat wimmen fer fatter wimmen. Y'all familiar with that there kind of trash? Purty young thing livin' in a ole haunted house on a foggy seacoast an' fallin' head over heels in love with some heavy-hung French pirate what drops anchor in th' cove now an' agin."

"I've seen it around. Titles like *The House on Gallows Hill* and *The Black Curse of Bleak Mansion*. That the stuff?"

"You hit it. Wall, she got herself tangled up with a couple or three scatterbrains what is tryin' to write an' now I reckon she done caught th' fever herself."

"These people ever do anything that was published?"

"Yeah, 'way back afore th' wheel got invented one of 'em writ somethin' what got put out by Water Moccasin Press down in th' Everglades or someplace. She claims to be a born-again Christian but she doan believe in th' Millennium or speakin' in tongues an' there ain't no way nobody kin be a born-again Christian lessen they believes in th' Millennium an' speakin' in tongues."

I said, "I wouldn't know. Look, Reverend, I can't stop your wife from wanting to write. It's something I've always wanted to do myself. It's just about incurable."

"You ever git published?"

"Once. A short story. Never came close since."

"What kind of stuff did you write?"

"About what you'd expect. Detectives, secret agents, master criminals, that sort of thing."

"Uh-huh. Wall, doan git me wrong, Lassiter, I ain't fightin' th' writin'. Thass prob'ly harmless enough. It's th' other stuff what got me worried."

ROSS H. SPENCER

"Such as?"

Huskin's granite jaw jutted. "Such as my wife sneakin' in after midnight 'bout oncet a month. Such as her hair bein' all topsy-turvy ever' so offen an' her bein' mebbe a couple sheets to th' wind an' juss a mite on th' smart-mouth side. Y'all follerin' me?"

I nodded. We were rapidly approaching a fork in the road and I was trying to anticipate Huskin's choice of direction. I said, "Where are these meetings held?"

"All over. They moves 'em aroun', residence to residence. Gen'rally speakin' I git outten th' house when they comes my direction."

"Does this organization have a name?"

"They calls themselves th' 'Blotters Club.' I looked in on 'em oncet when they was down in our rumpus room. They starts things out with th' club cheer an' then they sings th' club song an' they gits limbered up by playin' pin-th'-tail-on-th'-donkey an' juss laughin' an' screamin' fitten to wake up th' dead. After that they has coffee an' cake an' one of 'em hauls out somethin' she writ durin' th' week an' she reads it right out loud, this here gobbledygook 'bout winds in th' sycamores an' full moons an' lost loves an' ghosts flittin' ever' whichaway an' owls hootin' an' dogs howlin' an' ole fambly curses and all that there kind of carryin' on."

I whistled. "Thrill a minute outfit. Next thing you know they'll be into shuffleboard."

Huskin said, "There ain't never been nothin' out of line ever happened at my place but I ain't fixin' to bet th' outhouse on what might be gittin' pulled off somewheres else. My wife is considerable younger'n me an' th' Devil got th' whole Chicago area by th' short hair on a downhill pull. Juss ain't no tellin' what could be goin' on."

"And you want me to check it out."

"Wall, glory, brother, y'all ain't up here to pick no daffydills!" He chuckled. He liked that one. So did I. He'd taken the right direction.

I said, "Can you give me a jumping-off place?"

"Wall, they's a meetin' tonight."

"Would you describe Mrs. Huskin, please?"

16

MONASTERY NIGHTMARE

"Doan got no pitcher with me but she's, oh fav-fav, I reckon. Goes lak mebbe one-twenny, give or take a speck. Got sort of auburn color hair an' brown eyes, real humdinger, I allus thought. Drives a powder-blue Mercedes-Benz convertible automobile which I never should of give her. Put her smack-dab in th' way of temptation is what I prob'ly done."

"You'll want me to tag her from your residence?"

"Wall, hallelujah, brother, juss where else would y'all be 'spectin' to find her?" He slapped his knee and cackled a good old country boy cackle. All of a sudden Reverend Johnny Huskin was a barrel of laughs and I was breathing free and easy for the first time since his telephone call.

I said, "What time does she leave on meeting nights?"

"Few minnits after six-thirty. Allus travels west towards Ole Brasham Road. Y'all park a piece east of th' house an' track her an' keep me right up to snuff as th' evenin' goes along." He pushed a typewritten slip of paper across the desk to me. "This here's my address an' phone number. I gonna be home all night long." I tucked the paper into my shirt pocket without looking at it. Huskin said, "Y'all bill me here at th' office only make real certain y'all marks it 'personal.' " He paused and turned a hard, bright blue-eyed stare on me. He said, "Y'know, Lassiter, I'm a man of God. I got called to th' ministry by God an' I walks th' way He shows me to walk. He's a light unto my feet an' He doan want me to hurt nobody no way but I gonna tell y'all flat-out, a feller what messes with my wife is takin' some mighty serious chances with his good health 'cause I'd kill me a man lak that real sudden an' y'all better believe it."

I believed it. I knew the southern boys. With them it's don't kick my dog an' keep your cotton-pickin' paws offen my ole woman.

Huskin stood to terminate the conversation. We shook hands and I went out. He'd had one helluva grip. The kind you'd expect from an honest man, not from a scripture-spouting spiritual shill.

As I waited for the elevator I could hear Mt. Everest at the console saying, "Praise the Lord, Johnny Huskin Evangelistic Association . . . Yes, sir, we welcome contributions."

Ross H. Spencer

The faraway chimes were playing "We'll Say Good Night Here but Good Morning Up There." The song took me back across the years to the funeral of an old army buddy. He'd been shot for shacking with a civilian's wife.

We'd been stationed in Georgia at the time.

6

I put away a double cheeseburger and a bottle of beer at a Greek restaurant in Schiller Park before swinging from Irving Park Road onto northbound 294. The rush-hour traffic was clearing and I drove the dozen or so miles to White Birch Knolls in fifteen minutes. I tooled my battered Chevy Caprice slowly through the ultra-exclusive suburb and the prestige closed in on me like a shroud. It was nothing short of stifling. Eight-acre lots, four-car garages and not a house with less than ten rooms. Cadillacs, Porsches, Imperials, Ferraris, split-rail fences, twin tennis courts, Olympic-size swimming pools, vast green expanses of perfectly manicured lawn, long double-laned blacktop driveways winding through birch, pin oak, pine, sugar maple, magnolia, red bud and Russian olive. The Garden of Eden, twentieth-century style. A half million might have gotten a man into White Birch Knolls but he'd have been kept mighty busy reaching back for more. Kelton Blaylock, President of Dearborn Trust and Savings, lived there. So did Blake Ashhurst, the nine-hundred-thousand-dollar-a-season center fielder of the New York Yankees. Also Giuseppe Cosentino, owner of one of Chicago's largest grocery chains, and Kathleen Morehead, founder of the Dear Doris Cosmetics line. I wondered if rain dared descend on White Birch Knolls without written permission from its residents.

I passed the big crab orchard stone mansion on Raccoon Drive, traveled half a block, turned around and drove back to park where I was certain Johnny Huskin would be able to see my car from his house. Any man who'd go to the mat over a couple of bucks in gasoline money was a lead-pipe cinch to be checking me out. My watch said 6:16 when I killed the engine, lit a cigarette and leaned back to listen to one of those asinine phone-in chatter shows, the kind that attracts fifty-five-year-old broads who get their jollies by asking the guy at the microphone if oral sex is really all it's cracked up to be. Just as if they hadn't known since Roosevelt steamrollered Wendell Willkie. Or maybe Alf Landon. The giggling, gurgling proprietor of this particular dung heap was assuring a caller that all was not yet lost, that this season's Chicago Cubs could still emerge as divisional championship contenders providing that their hitting, pitching and fielding abilities proved to be of a quality that would enable them to emerge as divisional championship contenders. This succulent sports profundity thoroughly digested, I turned off the radio to focus my attention on the powder-blue Mercedes-Benz convertible that was easing from the white brick-edged driveway of the Huskin residence. When it headed west I started the Chevy and left the curb, flicking a glance at Reverend Johnny Huskin standing at the picture window of his palatial White Birch Knolls home. His Eye is on the Sparrow and I Know He Watches Me. With binoculars, yet.

Mrs. Huskin's Mercedes spun south on Old Brasham Road and she kicked it in the ass. She was a fast, skillful driver with an excellent eye for traffic openings. I managed to stay with her until she buzzed across an intersection on the yellow, leaving me screeched to a halt, staring at a red light.

I watched her expensive vehicle gallop into the distance and, when the signal flashed green, I continued southward on Old Brasham Road as far as Tuttle Avenue. There I pulled into the parking lot of Griswold's Bar and Liquors. I went in, used the washroom, drank two bottles of Stroh's, talked with Sam Blake the bartender for a few minutes, bought a carton of Marlboros and sauntered out to my Chevy. I picked up southbound 294 and drove homeward at a pace too leisurely to be associated with the hot pursuit of a fleeing quarry.

7

She was too young to have remembered the tune from its days of popularity but "Street of Dreams" was her favorite song and it was oozing from the record player as I opened the door to my second floor northwest side apartment. I took one look, tossed my carton of cigarettes onto the couch and braced myself. Here she came. She hit me head-on and very hard. She was a little tigress, squirming, panting, warm, soft, fragrant, but under her wonderful velvet she was wound tight and I knew that she had claws. She wore nothing but her half-slip and her red spike-heeled pumps. Her pink nipples drilled the front of my sports jacket, her auburn hair brushed my chin, her breath was sweet and hot on my neck. She said, "Oh, Jesus H. Christ, Luke, four weeks is a long time!"

I squeezed her and said, "Ain't it the truth?"

I tilted her head back and kissed her and when she'd taken her tongue out of my mouth she nibbled gently on my lower lip and mumbled, "Mmmm-m-m-m, my, but you're delicious!"

I grasped her shoulders and held her away from me at arm's length. I said, "Now listen to me! Just where the hell are you supposed to be this evening?"

She failed to sense the urgency in my voice. She winked an impish brown eye and grinned. "At a club meeting. Don't worry, baby, I'm covered."

"Where is the club meeting? What kind of house is it? What color?"

"It's 1201 Chestnut Lane in Park Ridge. Neat, beige-brick

Cape Cod with two enormous evergreens in the front yard. Our meetings are held in the family room."

"Where's the family room?"

"In the back of course. What's wrong?"

I put a finger to my lips for silence and said, "This." I walked to the phone, picked it up and dialed. I said, "Reverend Huskin?"

Huskin's voice rasped from the receiver. "This you, Lassiter?"

"Right. Reverend, your wife is at 1201 Chestnut Lane in Park Ridge. Sharp beige-brick Cape Cod with a couple big evergreens out front. Everything's kosher. I went around back and peeked through the window. They're in the family room."

"Who's in th' fambly room?"

"Your wife and some other women."

"Has she done anythin' wrong yet?"

"Well, yes, as a matter of fact, she has. She pinned the donkey's tail on its nose."

"Wall, looky, Lassiter, y'all foller her home anyways, juss in case. Check?"

"Check. I'll call you if she makes a stop. No stop, no call, okay, Reverend?"

"Okay, Lassiter." He was nervous. He was breathing like a man who'd just run the hundred all-out.

I said, "I'm phoning from a service station and I'd better get back." I hung up.

Barbara Huskin was staring at me with huge, uncomprehending eyes. She said, "Luke, what the hell was *that* all about?"

I said, "I just reported in to the client who hired me this afternoon. My client seems to be of the opinion that his wife may be getting a little action on the side."

She lifted a hand, traffic-cop style. "Wait a minute! *He* hired *you* to follow *me*? I don't believe this!"

"Well, sweetie, you damn well *better* believe it!"

"But why *you*, of all people?"

"Because I was located closest to his offices. We're mighty lucky that I was."

"Oh, dear God, *yes*!" She sagged onto the arm of my sofa and sat there, hands clenched tightly, shaking her head. I went into the kitchen and made a pair of ginger ale highballs. When I came back she was still perched on the sofa arm. She looked up blankly, accepting her drink and nipping at it in silence. I turned off the record player and sat in an armchair, watching her, feeling the pressure build. Suddenly she said, *"Damn!"* Just one word but packed with enough venom to poison *Roget's Thesaurus*.

I said, "It wouldn't be a bad idea to polish your rearview mirror."

She said, "Why, the sonofabitch! The double-talking, holier-than-thou, sneaking, snooping, spying, prying sonofa*bitch!"* Barbara Huskin popped to her feet as though she'd been sitting on a charcoal brazier. She tilted her glass and drained it without pausing for air. She dropped her black half-slip to the floor and stepped clear of it. She kicked it across the room and whirled to face me, stark naked, hands on her hips, legs slightly spread, pink-tipped breasts jutting, brown eyes blazing, shameless and ferocious. She said, "Luke Lassiter, take me to bed! Tonight you're in for one helluva trip!"

8

She was as good as her word. Always dynamite in bed, this time she chucked the record book out the window. It was approaching midnight when I said, "Barb, you'd better saddle up and ride. Your old man will be walking the floor."

She rolled away from me to sit on the edge of the bed with her head in her hands. She was trembling. She'd pulled all the stops. She said, "Luke, where the hell are my clothes?"

I reached for my cigarettes on the nightstand, lit a pair and handed one to her. I said, "Well, let's see. Your half-slip's somewhere in the living room, your dress is in the kitchen, your brassiere's in the bathroom and your panties are on the hallway chandelier."

"That figures. I was in heat."

"I don't have the foggiest notion about your shoes."

"I'm wearing them. Didn't have time to take them off."

"That may just explain the dents in my back."

Barb reached to rumple my hair. She said, "Yes, but I don't believe it accounts for all those claw marks on your shoulders."

"Barroom fight."

"Horse crap."

I piled out of bed and went through the apartment, harvesting Barb's clothing an item at a time. I stacked it on the bed and sat beside her, putting an arm around her bare shoulders. I said, "Care to tell me about the Blotters Club?"

She glanced up. "Johnny mentioned it?"

I nodded. "Do you really want to be a writer?"

She threw back her head and laughed. "Oh, my God, no! It's

MONASTERY NIGHTMARE

just that Johnny keeps such a close eye on me and the Blotters Club serves to get me a few evenings out. Candy Stoneman and I joined it last fall. Candy wangled us in."

"What's it all about?"

"Well, there are these two frustrated old biddies, Elizabeth Fudge and Geraldine Swisher. Swisher hasn't written anything, but Fudge wrote a book that was published back in the stone ages, *How to Be a Christian Although Happily Married*. It was well accepted, according to Fudge."

"By whom?"

"Orville Hobart said it was essential reading for married couples. He said it wouldn't hurt unmarried couples either."

"Who's Orville Hobart?"

"The pastor of the Apostolic Church of Heaven Eternal."

"That's the joint with the two-million-dollar pipe organ?"

"Yes. If it's played at maximum volume it registers on seismographs."

"I'll bet that impresses God all to hell. There were only two members in this club?"

"Uh-huh, just Fudge and Swisher. Fudge is an egomaniac and Swisher is a research fiend. Swisher researches every damned thing in sight. They'll be good friends until Swisher gets something published. Fudge can't stand competition. We hold meetings once a week at members' homes. Can you take it from there?"

"Sure. The Blotters Club is a front for you and Candy Stoneman. Candy swings, too."

"Oh, does she ever! Both of us attend the meetings at Fudge's and Swisher's but I never go to Candy's house and she's been to mine only once."

"Cute. If your husband calls Candy's house tonight he gets, 'Oh, certainly, Reverend Huskin, Barbara's in attendance this evening but she just ran down to the corner to pick up a pizza for the girls.' "

"Something like that. If he wants me to call him back Candy buzzes me here and I use your telephone."

"Or if he shows up at Candy's she tells him that you just went home with a migraine headache."

25

ROSS H. SPENCER

"Right. Then Candy calls me at your place and I light out for the tall timber. It works both ways."

"Don't Fudge and Swisher smell a rat?"

"Fudge and Swisher are in a fog. Anyway, they don't come into contact with our husbands. Mr. Stoneman gets out of the house because he can't stand Swisher. Johnny makes himself scarce because he loathes Fudge."

"Something to do with the Millennium, no doubt."

"Yes, that and speaking in tongues."

"Have you and Candy identified your boyfriends?"

"Never. We have nothing but telephone numbers."

"A phone number can be traced."

"Not yours. Your home number's unlisted."

"Doesn't matter. I know a guy who'll run down any number in the country for twenty-five bucks." I put out my cigarette and said, "Barb, you're forming a pattern and Huskin is beginning to sniff it out. He doesn't know what he has but he knows he has *some*thing. One night a month you come home looking like you've been dragged through a knothole. You'll have to be damned careful in the future. Want one for the road?"

"Christ, yes! A strong one!" When I returned with the drinks Barb said, "I just can't get over Johnny calling your office. That's a ten-thousand-to-one shot."

"Not really. I doubt that there are that many private investigations outfits in the whole country. I checked the Yellow Pages and he's right. I'm closest to him."

Barb worked on her highball for a couple of minutes. Then she said, "Once Elizabeth brought up the possibility of inviting a private detective to a Blotters Club meeting."

"What the hell for?"

"To gain knowledge of the ins and outs of the trade. Swisher went along with the idea. Swisher's for anything that comes under the heading of research."

I said, "Hold it right there, foxy! In the event you get tripped up you'll explain it by saying that you've been trying to get me to sit in with the girls for an evening?"

"It's weak, but it's better than no explanation at all. I can say that I've adopted the project as my own and that I've been

MONASTERY NIGHTMARE

keeping after you. You've been hard to persuade but you're weakening."

"Maybe you really should take up writing."

Barb stood to sort out her things. She was a beautiful woman, prettier stripped than when clothed and you just don't meet that kind every day in the week. At least I don't. She backed up to me and I hooked her brassiere clasp. She turned to give me a wry little smile. "Don't worry, Luke, everything's okay. It's just that an ounce of prevention is worth a pound of cure. Johnny's an absolute crank on the subject of fidelity. He might kill somebody."

"Yeah. Guess who."

She shook her head. "No, this is for the best. Now we're alerted. It's good that he picked you for his bloodhound."

I watched Barbara Huskin slip into her tight red panties with the big black butterfly on the fanny. I said, "Probably."

But it wasn't.

9

We'd talked about it, Barb and I. She was out of the Duluth, Minnesota, area and she'd been a highly impressionable nineteen-year-old waitress when Johnny Huskin had first visited the truck stop restaurant where she was employed. He'd been preaching at a tent meeting down the road. He'd been thirty-nine at the time, handsome, masculine, forceful, and Barb had fallen like a teenage load of bricks. When the revival meeting left town Johnny Huskin had himself a bride.

They'd known lean times but Huskin was a bulldog. He'd hung on. His recordings had grown popular, his television ministry had caught fire and Barb's role in his life had gotten smaller and smaller. "I'm like a goddam show horse," she'd told me. "Johnny walks me around the ring a couple of times and kicks my ass back into my stall." I hadn't said much about it but Huskin had a point. Barb was a heavy smoker, she drank on occasion and a cuss word would slip out now and then. It would be difficult for a nationally known evangelist to put such a wife on display whether he loved her or not. So Huskin had been swept away by his pursuit of acclaim and his wife had ended up in the hay with another guy. *Several* other guys, I had no doubt. She certainly knew what mattresses were for.

Once I'd said, "I suppose he just got lost on that sawdust trail."

Barb had said, "Whatever. The bottom line is that I can't stand the sanctimonious bastard."

"Then why don't you pitch it and walk?"

"Luke, you don't know Johnny Huskin. He'd track me down and kill the man I'm with."

28

MONASTERY NIGHTMARE

"What man? There wouldn't have to be a man. Just get a nice clean divorce and you're out with half."

"Half? Half of zero? Everything's tied up in that damned evangelistic association account. The evangelistic association owns our house, it even owns my goddam *automobile*!" Her brown eyes had narrowed to slits.

I'd said, "And Huskin *is* the evangelistic association?"

"He signs the checks."

"What if he drops dead?"

"Then there are arrangements for control of the account to pass to me. Are you suggesting something?"

"Not me! If you want him dead, screw him to death."

Her laugh had been short and sharp. "I get sex from Johnny Huskin once every three months and it's like being mounted by a cigar store Indian."

"You're in between a rock and a hard place."

"Yes, but, Luke, that's a position I have to defend. I have eleven years of my life invested in Johnny Huskin. I can remember cooking on a rooming-house hot plate in Tomah, Wisconsin, when he was singing and preaching for twenty-five dollars a night. I'm going to stick it out because there has to be well over a million in that bank account."

I'd whistled and Barb had dropped the subject.

I fluffed up my pillow and stretched out. Somewhere in the twilight area that borders sleep I weighed my situation. I got along with Barbara Huskin, she was one helluva roll in the clover and she'd never cost me a dime. But I didn't love her, she didn't love me, and she was a woman whose husband had a fidelity complex and a gun collection.

It didn't quite balance out.

10

*B*arb had put me through the mill. I slept late and reached my office at 10:45. I checked the telephone-answering box. There was a single message and I recognized the voice instantly. It belonged to Buck Westerville and he told me that if I had no other plans he'd be over to see me between eleven and noon. Buck Westerville was a born hustler. He could sniff out a rapid dollar in twenty acres of rotten cabbage. I'd met him in Vietnam where he'd swiped a U.S. Army jeep and traded it for six cases of Japanese whiskey. Then he'd peddled the booze for seven hundred dollars, ran the seven hundred to more than four grand in a series of dice games and lost every dime of it playing poker.

But, whatever he was, Buck was no quitter and he'd never given up on hitting the big lick that would put him on top of the heap. He'd booked horses, operated a lonely hearts service, sold half-acre Texas Panhandle "ranch" sites and served as a free-lance stock market consultant. These ventures had failed and more recently Buck had become a tracer of missing persons. Apparently he'd made a good thing of it. "Anybody Anywhere Anytine." That was the slogan on the door of his fancy office on Wacker Drive. Buck's secretary had blamed the sign-painter for the "Anytine." The sign-painter had insisted that he'd painted exactly what the secretary had typed. The secretary had called the sign-painter a liar. The sign-painter had called the secretary a whore. Three weeks later they'd been married. They'd bought a delicatessen up on Foster Avenue and they'd put up a big sign. JOE AND BERTHA'S DELACOTESSAN. I notice things like that. I'm a detective.

MONASTERY NIGHTMARE

Buck was making money and he never dirtied his hands in the process. He didn't have to. Buck had connections. With the proper connections just about anybody can become a United States senator. Take a look at the record.

Buck worked for fraud victims, anguished parents, jilted lovers, insurance companies, collection agencies, foreign governments, the Mafia, anybody who'd pay his fee. He distributed his assignments among small-timers like myself, men familiar with the places and faces of Chicago, men whose knowledge saw to it that Missing Person #123 entered his hotel to be greeted by the wife he'd walked out on back in Baltimore. Or a bullet. Whichever way it went it didn't matter to Buck Westerville. Mention ethics to Buck and he thought you had a 1927 automobile and a lithp.

He stepped into my office, a bulky, red-faced, perspiring man of about forty-five years, sleek dark-haired, bulldog visaged with bright, quick eyes darting behind thick-lensed tortoiseshell spectacles. He wore a handsomely cut, pin-striped dark blue suit, white shirt, baby-blue necktie, and there was a small gold cross affixed to a lapel. The cross amused me. A cross on Buck Westerville's lapel was like a Star of David on Adolf Hitler's. He was a bachelor man-about-town and a devil with the ladies. He belonged to the best clubs, frequented the finest restaurants and held season tickets for everything from football to hopscotch. Buck Westerville literally oozed prestige. He chucked his seventy-five-dollar pearl-gray hat onto my battered leatherette couch, brushed sweat from his forehead and said, "Luke, your fucking elevator's busted."

I said, "They told me they'd fix it on Friday."

Buck said, "Which Friday?"

I said, "Last Friday."

Our handshake was perfunctory and Buck occupied the straight-backed wooden chair near my desk. He said, "How's it going?"

I said, "Nothing worth writing home about. Chronic malnutrition and my bubonic plague acts up from time to time."

"I thought it was leprosy."

"I got over the leprosy. Went to a chiropractor."

"Been a while, Luke. How long now?"

31

ROSS H. SPENCER

"The Crystal Ball thing."

"That's right. Crystal Ball. You were damned good in that matter. My thanks."

"I got paid."

"Oh, you most certainly did! You know, Luke, there was no iron-clad rule that said you had to jump into bed with her the very moment you found her."

I said, "It wasn't the very moment I found her. It was five, maybe ten minutes later."

Buck didn't say anything.

I said, "You see, Crystal's a bit flighty and that was the only way I could get her attention."

"By the way, she's gone again."

"When did she fly the coop?"

"This morning, according to Itchy."

"Itchy?"

"Itchy Balzino."

"The Mafia wheel?"

"That's him."

I shook my head. "My God, and I'm still *alive*?"

"No problem. Itchy's broad-minded."

"Uh-huh. Well, I'm not tracking Crystal Ball again."

"You won't have to. Itchy figures she's just gotta get it out of her system. He told me he's gonna let her ramble until she runs out of gas."

"Which will be about forty years after the Second Coming of Christ."

"Itchy says he's all fed up with hearing Crystal recite Shakespeare and rave about the detective who found her during that last AWOL."

I said, "I can understand the part about Shakespeare but we were in bed less than two hours."

Buck winked at me. He said, "The Japs bombed Pearl Harbor for less than two hours." He put a match to his vile-smelling corncob pipe. It was a macho stage prop with Buck, just as it had been with General MacArthur. He peered at me through the smoke. "Crystal Ball called my office an hour ago. She booked a Monday morning appointment. Wouldn't it be funny if she was looking for you?"

MONASTERY NIGHTMARE

I chuckled an uneasy chuckle. "Forget it. Crystal Ball eats licorice in *bed!*"

Buck stretched and yawned, a mannerism indicating that he was about to get down to brass tacks. He said, "Doing much reading these days?"

I said, "I keep *Newsweek* and the *Guinness Book of Records* in the bathroom."

"You read a lot in 'Nam. What happened? Got a broad in your hair?"

"No, I kicked the habit."

"Broads?"

"Reading."

"You were a Carl Garvey fan, as I recall."

"Yeah, I've read everything he wrote. Started in high school. I liked Garvey better than any of the Chicago area writers."

"You forget Hemingway?"

"No, but I'm trying."

"Garvey was okay but he had no message."

"Well, of *course* he had no message! Jesus Christ, Buck, Garvey wrote to *entertain!* He wasn't deep and he didn't mean to be! If I want a goddam message I'll read Thomas Aquinas!"

Buck leaned forward in his chair, elbows on his knees. He said, "Do you recall the details of his death?"

I squinted. "They're a bit fuzzy. Didn't he die while on his way to Naples to patch up a rift in the church, something between the Latins and the Greeks?"

"Not Thomas Aquinas, Luke. Carl Garvey."

"Oh. Yeah, last fall they found his sailboat abandoned way the hell out on Lake Michigan."

"Right, and on a relatively calm day. Garvey was supposed to be an all-weather sailor. Struck me as being a bit odd."

"I don't think so. Nobody beefed. He'd had a heart attack earlier in the year."

Buck gave me a long contemplative look. He said, "Luke, you've done some writing."

"Sure. Even had an agent. Sold one short story. That's writing?"

"You threw in the towel?"

"Practically. Why whip a dead horse?"

33

Ross H. Spencer

"What kind of story did you sell?"

"A whodunnit. 'Lilacs Are Fatal.' Jackpot. Two hundred bucks. The agent got twenty and I drank up the rest in a week."

Buck frowned at my faded office carpeting. Then he looked up. "Do me a favor, Luke?"

I said, "Maybe. On three conditions. If there's money in it, if it's kosher and if Crystal Ball isn't involved."

Buck stared at me. Stonily. He rose abruptly and took his hat from my couch. He said, "Luke, there just ain't no Santa Claus."

"Then skip it. I'm too damn old to go to jail."

Buck laughed. It was an odd, lurching sound, like a cross between a cough and a burp. "It wasn't all that serious. I just wanted you to write something for me."

I shrugged the shrug of a compromised man. "I believe I could listen to that. I'm down to neck bones."

"Not now, Luke. Have lunch with me at the Pelican Club on Monday and we'll kick it around over a steak." He peeled a pair of fifties from a green bundle the diameter of a rolled rump roast. He placed them carefully on a corner of my desk and said, "That's good-faith money. See you Monday." He left my office, taking with him the greatest opportunity of my lifetime, and I let him go without protest.

No is a two-letter adverb used to express the negative of an alternative choice or possibility. It's one of the shortest words in the English language, it hardly ever gets a man into trouble, and I rarely use it.

11

*C*rystal Ball. What an uninhibited and thoroughly likable blonde minx. I'd stepped into her room at the Tomahawk Motel on North Avenue and found her sprawled naked on the bed, gnawing on a licorice twist and poring over a volume of Shakespeare. She didn't so much as blink at my intrusion. I'd said, "Crystal Ball?"

She'd said, "Yes, and you're Inspector McVickers from Scotland Yard."

I'd said, "No, I'm Luke Lassiter from West Adams Street. Don't you think you should get dressed?"

"Why? Are you embarrassed?"

"Not at all. Aren't you?"

"Well, look at it this way—if I were embarrassed I'd get dressed."

I'd looked around and said, "Who's with you?"

"Just Shakespeare. Want some licorice?"

I'd stepped to the phone and called Buck Westerville. He'd told me to hold the fort until he could arrange for transportation. When I'd hung up she was standing at my elbow. She'd said, "You're a very special person."

"How can you tell?"

"By your aura."

"What color is it?"

"I don't know. It's a brand-new color. How do you describe a brand-new color?"

"I've never seen a brand-new color."

"Speaking of colors, I'm not a true blonde."

35

"Yes, I'd noticed. It isn't important."

"Good. How soon will they come for me?"

"I have no idea."

"An hour?"

"Depends. Longer, I'd imagine."

She was unbuttoning my shirt. "We'll have time, won't we?"

"More than likely."

Two hours later a couple of guys had pulled up in a black Cadillac and tooted the horn. Crystal Ball had dressed hurriedly, tucked Shakespeare under her arm and smiled sadly. She'd said, "If we do meet again, why, we shall smile! If not, why then, this parting was well made."

I'd said, "Is that right?"

"It's from Shakespeare. *Julius Caesar.*"

"Okay."

She'd kissed me on the nose. "You're even more special than I'd thought."

The phone jolted me back to the present. It was Reverend Johnny Huskin. He said, "Lassiter, I juss wanted to say y'all done real good lass night."

"Thanks, Reverend. There really wasn't much to it. I followed her until she turned into your driveway." I'd done nothing of the sort. I'd been asleep ten minutes after she'd left my apartment. I said, "I don't believe that you have a problem there. She seems to be behaving herself."

"Yeah, reckon as how thass true. Y'all know a feller juss cain't help sittin' aroun' thinkin'. Ever juss sit aroun' thinkin', Lassiter?"

"About what?"

"Oh, ever'thin'."

"No, Reverend, not everything. I'm not that good."

Huskin chuckled. "Wall, now, y'all know what I mean. Y'all married, Lassiter?"

"Not anymore."

"But y'all was?"

"Long time ago."

"What happened?"

"What didn't?"

"Bad?"

MONASTERY NIGHTMARE

"Not good."

"Y'all got a lady friend?"

"Yeah, sort of. Don't see much of her."

"Wall, thass probly on account of y'all bein' so busy trailin' people an' stuff lak that."

"Probably, yes."

"Y'all ever sit aroun' thinkin' 'bout a woman?"

"Yes, in fact you just caught me in the act."

"Reckon y'all know how it goes then."

"Maybe not. Different women, different thoughts."

"Lassiter, a woman kin tear up a man's mind somethin' fierce."

"Depends on the man, depends on the woman."

Huskin cleared his throat. Over the phone it sounded like a volcanic eruption. Here it came. He'd been stretching the conversation because there was something on his mind. He said, "Looky, Lassiter, this here ain't hardly no proper matter to be discussin' with a almost total stranger but when y'all gits right down to it there ain't nobody else I kin take it up with."

"Go right ahead, Reverend."

"Wall, y'all see, sometimes my wife wears these here red panties what got this here big black butterfly on."

I said, "I don't believe I'm in a position to comment on that."

" 'Course not but th' funny thing is this here big black butterfly is in *front* an' when she come home lass night it was in *back*. Now what y'all think of *that*?"

"I think she probably put her, uhh-h-h, panties on backwards before she left the house."

"Yeah, reckon thass what happened. She seemed in a turrble hurry to be gittin' on her way. Besides there juss ain't no way she could of got 'em turned aroun' whilst she was playin' pin-th'-tail-on-th'-donkey, now is there?"

I managed a weak laugh. "None that comes readily to mind."

There was a lengthy silence before Huskin said, "Lassiter, y'all seems lak a real nice feller. Mebbe juss a mite on th' brash side but y'all comes on a heap straighter than most. Ever been a Christian?"

"Not that I know of."

ROSS H. SPENCER

"Thass somethin' a man never fergits. Mebbe we kin talk on it sometime."

I said, "We'll see." I excused myself and hung up.

That imperious air of authority had left Johnny Huskin and he was just another country boy with a case of the dark-blue blues. A man can slip into that mood when he senses things that he really isn't certain of, when he's whistling in the dark. Huskin had a beautiful, passionate wife but he'd alienated her. He had a national television audience of more than twenty million people but he was lonely. He preached the teachings of Jesus Christ but he wouldn't have known Him if they'd met in a telephone booth. My heart went out to the poor bastard.

12

I went down to the Sherwood to drink it over and spotted Kenny Blossom talking to Nick Spanzetti at the newsstand. What was worse, Kenny Blossom spotted *me*. He yelled, "Hey, Luke!" I pretended not to hear and went down the steps. That wouldn't help, he'd be right on my heels. Mary O'Rourke looked up with her bright, lopsided smile and said, "Wanna discuss etchings?"

I glanced over my shoulder and said, "Cool it! Mucho Macho will be right in."

Mary made a face and we watched Kenny Blossom shoulder his way into the Sherwood. He was a big, blubbery bastard, six-three or thereabouts, going something like 260 and softer than mush with a belly protruding balloonlike over a wide black leather belt bearing an enormous brass buckle with a bronc-buster and YAHOO stamped on it. Kenny was very much into the western thing. Along with the obnoxious belt buckle came a narrow-brimmed white Stetson, three-inch brass-studded leather wristbands and short-topped cowboy boots. He wore a fawn-colored western-cut denim jacket that sported seventeen miles of saddle stitching and his shirt was pink with imitation pearl snaps. Kenny's shirts were always pink. Or maybe it was always the same shirt. However it worked, the shirt blew his he-man image all to hell because if there's a color less masculine than pink I've never seen it.

He was the garrulous type with chronic diarrhea of the mouth and he took obvious delight in telling you just how much he knew about other people's business, including your own. He had kinky blond hair, watery-blue eyes and a face that resembled a meatloaf broadsided by a Greyhound bus. He smoked little Italian cigars, drank whatever the other guy would buy and he packed a .44 pearl-handled Colt six-shooter in a shoulder holster, leaving his jacket open so the weapon would properly impress those who were properly impressed by .44 pearl-handled Colt six-shooters. He was licensed to carry the weapon because he was a South State Street private detective with an eight-by-eight office at the back end of a peep-show establishment where a hundred bucks would get you an illegal tattoo of a fat woman copulating with anything from a Russian wolfhound to a three-headed dragon. Kenny's tattoo was on his left forearm, the fat broad was taking on a Brahma bull and, if I was any judge, the bull was getting the worst of it.

I'd never been able to understand how Kenny Blossom had managed to make a living in the field of private investigation. He had the tact of a drunken rhinoceros and he was about as inconspicuous as an aircraft carrier at a Baptist ice cream social. I hadn't seen him in weeks but my luck had just run out. Now he'd walk up, slap me on the shoulder and say, "Hiya, Luke, what's new?" Then he'd wait for me to buy.

Kenny walked up, slapped me on the shoulder, said, "Hiya, Luke, what's new?" and waited for me to buy.

I ordered a round of Stroh's and said, "Nothing much, Kenny, how's it with you?" I'd known him for years, I'd been to his house once, he'd stopped by my apartment on a couple of occasions and I'd thrown a few jobs his way, stuff too sleazy for me to handle, which is pretty sleazy, ask just about anybody.

Kenny said, "Oh, I'm keeping busy." His voice was an octave too high for his bulk and he wore a self-important little smirk when he had an iron in the fire. Apparently he had an iron in the fire.

I yawned and said, "You still working that hotel during conventions?"

Kenny chortled, a sound akin to that emitted by henhouses during invasions by Bengal tigers. "Naw, Luke, that was minor league crap. I'm on to something that'll pay real money if I play it right." If I was supposed to ask questions, I didn't. Every time I saw Kenny Blossom he was on to something that would pay real money if he played it right. He ogled Mary O'Rourke in her merry-men outfit and turned to me, rolling his wet blue eyes. Out of the side of his mouth he said, "Hey, Luke, you ever get around to working that over?"

I said, "Are you nuts? Her boyfriend's with the Mafia."

"What's his thing? Jukeboxes, towel supplies?"

"No, he shoots people."

"Oh-oh!"

I said, "Yeah, oh-oh." Kenny Blossom was right in form, boring the Christ out of me.

"So nothing happening, huh, Luke?"

"Playing a lot of solitaire."

"Win a few?"

"When I cheat." I had the feeling he was trying to get around to something. I sat in silence, listening to the backbar radio play Willie Nelson's version of "Georgia on My Mind." Willie Nelson singing "Georgia on My Mind" ran a distant second to a fucked-up locomotive whistle in a long, dark tunnel but it beat hell out of Kenny Blossom's inane chatter.

Kenny moved his barstool closer to mine and leaned toward me. There was a blotch of ketchup above his upper lip and he'd been eating onions. The self-important smirk slithered across his doughy features. He said, "Still living in the same place, Luke?"

"Best I can afford."

Kenny winked at me. "Getting much these days?"

I shrugged. "There's a couple blondes hanging around the Circus Tap. When one won't, the other will."

Kenny didn't say anything. He lit a short Italian cigar and blew a thin cloud of blue smoke at the ceiling. Whatever it had been, he'd lost the handle. I finished my beer and got up. I said, "Well, so long, Kenny, I gotta ramble."

"I thought you didn't have nothing cooking."

"I don't. I'm going home and hit the hay early."

Kenny leered. "You must of had a real rough night."

13

I bailed my car out of the Adams Street parking lot and drove north on the Outer Drive. Buck Westerville had flushed an ancient rabbit from the briar patch of my memory. As a teenager I'd read Carl Garvey's stuff voraciously. So voraciously that I'd been kicked out of English class. From her desk Miss Hadley had fixed me with a steely stare. She'd said, "Luke Lassiter, you aren't reading Charles Dickens. You're reading Carl Garvey again."

I'd said, "How do you know?"

Miss Hadley was a small woman with frizzy brown hair and a vastly superior smile. She'd smiled her vastly superior smile. She'd said, "Your hair is standing straight up."

I'd said, "But my hair always stands straight up. I got a crew cut."

Two detention periods. One for reading Carl Garvey in English class and one for introducing the subject of crew cuts. In those days the teachers were in charge and only the janitors wore blue jeans. Carl Garvey had been a young writer then, long on hyperbole and short on patience, but he'd improved with age, maturing into a tongue-in-cheek spellbinder. Garvey's hero, Hillary Condor, never failed to encounter the erotic and the macabre in staggering quantities. On the surface he was a nickel-and-dime divorce shamus much like myself, but Hillary Condor didn't freeze his cookies off in the January parking lots of cheap motels waiting for fat housewives to emerge from lustful romps with neighborhood pharmacists. Not the *real* Hillary Condor. Behind a sleazy facade the real Hillary Condor was

Monastery Nightmare

the United States Government's number-one troubleshooter, operating out of his luxurious West Virginia mountain retreat, Condor's Nest, which he shared with Miriam Mission, his beautiful, honey-blonde, lavender-eyed, oversexed secretary.

Condor drove a purple, souped-up Ferrari convertible, he owned a motorcycle powered by a turbo-charged 455 cubes V-8 engine and his heavily armed jet-black helicopter had reserved parking space on the roof of the Pentagon.

Hillary Condor spent his time indulging in sex orgies with gorgeous Eurasian double agents, dodging Soviet ambushes and thwarting plots to contaminate the North American hemisphere with deadly pollen from the rare African boomba-boomba plant developed to several hundred times its normal size in the secret Himalayan laboratories of the dreaded Dr. Boris Scraggovitch.

Carl Garvey's suave and brilliant operative was independently wealthy and on a first-name basis with the President of the United States. He was hung like a Percheron stud, he possessed the staying capabilities of a Sherman tank and he'd seduced women on every continent, not to mention a mind-boggling number at sea and in the air. He'd been known to strangle karate masters with their own black belts, he could scale skyscrapers without benefit of special equipment and on one occasion he'd swum the English Channel in white tie and tails to attend a full-dress society ball in Calais.

This sort of fiction sold: Hillary Condor's admirers had been legion and I was in its vanguard. I felt that I knew him personally. He became thoroughly predictable to me. I could sense, pages in advance, how Condor would respond to a budding situation, when he would lash out in his sudden, cold, lethal fury or when he would bide his time, awaiting a more advantageous position from which to crush the minions of evil.

I'd grown up, more or less, and, following hitches with the Army, the Merchant Marine and the Chicago Police Force, I'd borrowed money to open my private investigations agency on West Adams Street. I'd spent the early days hacking away at short stories because there hadn't been much business to attend to in the early days, a state of affairs that had persisted into the later days. Through it all I'd read Carl Garvey and I'd read *about* him and of his passion for sailing his *Miss Fortune*, the appropriately christened little craft that had carried him to his untimely demise. I'd read of Garvey's purchase of an abandoned old monastery on the Fox river some thirty miles west of Chicago and of how, when asked what he intended doing with an abandoned old monastery, Garvey had replied that he had no intentions of doing anything with it, that he'd bought it simply because he'd always wanted to own an abandoned old monastery.

The dust jackets of Garvey's books always carried the same photograph, that of a sandy-haired, pimply faced, receding-chinned man and it was extremely difficult to associate this Sunday School teacherish–appearing individual with the superhero tendencies of Hillary Condor. Still, it figured that Garvey must have been an accomplished hand with the ladies because, in his fifties, he'd taken a wife more than twenty years his junior. She was a raven-haired, blue-eyed knockout who'd surfaced occasionally in the Sunday newspaper profiles. She was an excellent bowler, a superb gymnast and swimmer, a white-water canoeist, a crack rifle shot, one helluva tennis player and she'd once reached the finals of the United States Olympic figure-skating trials. Aside from that she didn't have a great deal on the ball. She drove an Italian sports car, her name was Jennifer and she was making Carl Garvey deliriously happy.

Then, one morning in October, presumably before dawn, Garvey had tacked eastward out of Burnham Harbor and into the graying Lake Michigan horizon. At dusk the *Miss Fortune* had been found unoccupied and the incident had been attributed to probable cardiac arrest, this because he'd suffered a severe seizure during the previous spring.

I'd identified with Hillary Condor the way my father's generation had identified with Hopalong Cassidy and the loss of Carl Garvey had left a void. He'd departed the shabby little stage of my life and there'd been no curtain calls.

Not yet.

14

I swung west from the Outer Drive onto North Avenue. Christ, it was hot. Mother Nature is a crotchety old bat just about anywhere on the planet but she seems to save her wildest tantrums for Chicago, Illinois. In Chicago she runs amok. During the winter of '78–'79 she buries the city under more than eight feet of snow. Two years later she produces less than ten inches. She has hot spells for November and frosts for June. It's too wet or too dry, too cold or too damned hot and today it was too damned hot. Chicagoans just can't handle heat. They go crazy in it. They swing first and make inquiries later. They drive like maniacs, drink like water buffalo and murder one another with gay abandon. On a hot day Chicago is a very good place not to be.

Ahead of me the North Avenue blacktop shimmered in heat rivulets. To my left a hitchhiking teenage female shrieked a volley of obscenities at a white-haired old lady who shook her fist at the girl, lost control of her vehicle and plowed headlong into the tail end of a parked laundry truck. To my right a tavern door flew open and a pair of wild-eyed drunks spilled onto the sidewalk to commence beating the living bejesus out of each other. I turned north on Harlem Avenue and behind me a hefty bearded guy in a rusty gray van blew his horn repeatedly and waved me out of his way. I thumbed my nose into the rearview mirror. When he saw an opening he jammed his foot onto the accelerator, swung wide and went around me like an overdue meteor. He yelled, "Pull over, you dumb bastard!" I gave him the finger and wheeled west through the parking lot of the

Leffingwell Historical Museum to 72nd Court, where I parked in the alley beside Bessie Barnum's Circus Tap.

Bessie Barnum, the aging, portly gal who owned the joint, professed to be a distant relative of P. T. Barnum and the interior of the place was done in circus reds and yellows with old sideshow posters adorning the walls. Monstro the Mighty Midget, Oogli-Googli the Woman with the Forked Tongue, Colonel L. B. Judd and His Trained Great White Shark. I remembered none of these attractions but the pictures would have scared a bulldog off a gut-wagon. The jukebox was loaded with the music of circus bands and steam calliopes and it was belching "Thunder and Blazes" at the top of its lungs.

Bessie Barnum was standing at a table in the back, talking to Stash Dubinski. Bessie had the hots for Stash and she rarely missed an opportunity to be near him. Stash was a big guy with an underslung jaw and gentle brown eyes, a man who'd walk fifteen miles barefoot over broken glass to lend a friend a helping hand. I'd known him for years, long before he'd quit the Chicago force to become Security Chief at the Leffingwell Museum. He was a guy you could talk to, a man's man. He'd tell you his problems and he'd listen to yours, he'd drink your beer and he expected you to drink his. A long time ago we'd gotten into a lot of mischief and chased a lot of women and hoisted a lot of beers but we were older now, the mischief was behind us, so were most of the women and there wasn't much left but the beer. We were still pretty good with the beer. Bessie brought two bottles of Stroh's and I watched Stash down half of his at a single gulp. He wiped his mouth with the back of his hand and said, "First one today. Just got here. How did the Cubbies do?"

"Blew it in the ninth."

Stash smiled broadly. "Hey, geez, that's great! Them kids are showing promise! Last year they was blowin' 'em in the *first!*" Stash was a dyed-in-the-wool Cubs fan. Dyed-in-the-wool Cubs fans can find hope in a leper colony in the middle of a typhoon during a diphtheria epidemic.

I said, "Stash, you look all knocked out."

Stash motioned to Bessie for more beer. He yawned and nodded. "Yeah, well, Luke, that ain't exactly no accident. Leffingwell's a disaster area right now. Everybody's running in

MONASTERY NIGHTMARE

circles. Couple weeks ago we got Rabies Razzano's 1932 Packard. Razzano held up twenty banks with that old wagon. Then, last Friday, we got William Tell's bow and a quiver of his arrows."

I frowned. I said, "How can you be sure that it's William Tell's stuff?"

"Oh, easy! There's a dried-up apple core stuck on one of the arrows."

I nodded. "That clinches it."

"Sure, but that ain't all. This morning those blinkety-blank Red Sea Documents arrived and we're gonna be stuck with 'em clean through the first of the year."

"Red Sea Documents?"

Stash looked horrified. "You never heard of the Red Sea Documents? Why them old papers are the hottest historical find since they located the ship that never returned." He tilted his bottle and polished it off. "You know, I always wondered where the sonofabitch went."

I said, "Hell, I didn't even know it was gone."

Bessie came with our fresh round. Stash said, "Well, that's the tricky part, Luke. It *wasn't* gone. It never *left*. It was sitting at some old pier up in Boston for eighty-some years. They forgot to hoist the goddam anchor."

I said, "Well, Jesus Christ, why didn't somebody on the crew say something?"

"We'll never know. They all starved to death. It was in the papers a few weeks ago." I paid Bessie Barnum and she went away looking puzzled. Stash stared gloomily at the floor. He said, "Luke, I'm worried. I got three guards on vacation and I've heard stories that the Second United Atheists may try to steal the Red Sea Documents."

I said, "Pardon me. The Second United Who?"

"The Second United Atheists. They busted off from the First United Atheists a couple years back. Neither one of 'em believes in anything but they don't believe in anything in different ways, you see."

"Not exactly."

"Me neither, but I think they call it a dogmatic dispute."

"What's with these Red Sea Documents?"

47

"They're the records of some religious maniac named Barnaby Heffernan. Heffernan was all over the Holy Land back in the eighteen hundreds. He even discovered the place where Christ lost his moccasins."

I said, "You mean sandals, Stash."

Stash said, "Well, whatever."

I said, "Whaddaya mean 'whatever'? There's a difference! Sandals got straps!"

Stash said, "The documents are Barnaby Heffernan's personal account of his trip and all the places he visited and the people he met and the visions he saw and things like that."

I said, "Moccasins got beads."

Stash said, "Heffernan buried the documents down by the Red Sea some goddam place and nobody found 'em for about a hundred and fifty years."

I said, "When you get right down to it, neither is good for your feet. They got no support for the metatarsal arch."

Stash said, "They're priceless."

I said, "Well, I'd think so. Christ's sandals got to be worth a fortune."

Stash said, "Luke, I ain't talking about Christ's sandals. I'm talking about the Red Sea Documents."

"Well, what the hell happened to Christ's sandals?"

"Heffernan put 'em on and drowned trying to walk on water."

Stash looked around for Bessie. She'd been standing directly behind him, taking it all in. Stash said, "Give us another beer, Bessie."

Bessie shook her head. She said, "Sorry, boys, not another drop. You've had enough."

Somebody tapped me on the shoulder. I had company. The hefty, bearded guy who'd been driving the rusty gray van. The sonofabitch had tracked me. He said, "Care to step outside?"

I said, "Well, not really. It's awfully hot out there." I stood and busted him very hard on his beard. Stash helped me scrape him up and carry him to a booth.

Bessie Barnum was shaking her head. She said, "Luke, what the hell's wrong with you? I talked to that man when he came in. He just wanted to show you that your tailpipe had fallen off!"

15

I was hanging my jacket in my living room closet when the telephone rang. Barbara Huskin. I said, "Where are you calling from?"

"White Birch Knolls Pharmacy."

"Good. Not from the house anymore, Barb."

"Why? You think I'm bugged?"

"Could be. Any guy who'd hire a gumshoe might take it a step further."

"Luke, I talked to Elizabeth Fudge this morning. Next week's meeting's at her house and the club will pay your daily fee if you'll be our guest."

"I don't think so. I don't like Elizabeth Fudge and I haven't even met the woman."

"All you'd have to do is answer questions. Exaggerate. Throw in a couple of assassinations, a stakeout or so, maybe a kidnapping, sprinkle generously with blood and you'll have them standing on their ears."

"Not my idea of a lovely evening."

"Luke, it'd be excellent cover if Johnny ever learns that we've been in contact. It'd give me a way out. Do it for me, please!"

"Can I get a drink there?"

"Oh, my God, no! Not with Edgar on the premises!"

"Edgar?"

"Elizabeth's husband."

"What about Edgar? Does he bite?"

"No, Edgar drinks. Not often, but, when he does, it's 'Good morning, John, I brought your saddle home.' "

49

"Belligerent?"

"Nothing like that. It's just that when Edgar gets a few under his belt he thinks he's the Pope."

"Come on, Barb!"

"Honest to God! In his den Edgar has this enormous stereo rig, forty-eight-inch speakers and about a jillion watts per channel. He also has a recording of 'Ave Maria' played on that two-million-dollar pipe organ of the Apostolic Church of Heaven Eternal."

"And he plays this recording?"

"At full volume."

"Holy Christ! Which 'Ave Maria'?"

"Gounod's."

"I prefer Schubert's."

"So do I but you can't argue with the Pope. Edgar puts on a bed sheet and he goes around blessing people. Elizabeth will have a big bowl of fruit punch. Maybe you could bring your own bottle and spike your drinks on the sly."

"Will Candy Stoneman be there?"

"Yes, this meeting and the next. Then it'll be her night to howl. Hands off, please. Candy's quite a dish."

I thought about it. Who could say? I might learn something about writing. I overran my better judgment. I said, "Okay, I'll take a shot at it. What time and what's Fudge's address?"

"She lives in Elmwood Park. I'll pick you up at the Circus Tap about seven o'clock."

"Won't that be risky? Trucking me around in your automobile?"

"Not if I'm taking you to a Blotters Club meeting."

I said, "Oh, what a tangled web we weave."

Barb said, "When first we practice to survive."

"That doesn't rhyme."

Barb giggled. "No, but it works."

16

*I*t was a sunny Sunday morning. I was flopped on the couch, an ice bag on my head, a cigarette in my mouth and a can of Stroh's in my hand. I was having it out with a very hairy hangover and I had no one but myself to blame. The choice had been mine, Saturday night in Mary O'Rourke's bedroom or in Bessie Barnum's Circus Tap, drinking beer with Stash Dubinski. Six of one and half a dozen of the other. Clawed shoulders or a blinding headache. Mary O'Rourke didn't know when she'd had enough sex, Stash Dubinski didn't know when he'd had enough beer and keeping up with either was impossible.

I left the couch to switch the television selector to Johnny Huskin's UHF channel and returned with a groan. Only the ice bag was keeping the top of my head from flying off.

The Huskin program had been taped in Shreveport, Louisiana, a few weeks earlier on a weekend that Barbara Huskin and I had utilized to the fullest. The auditorium was jammed with hand-clapping foot-stompers and Johnny Huskin was seated at a piano on a stage banked high with red roses. He smiled and waved and the applause was deafening. He hit a few bluesy country chords on the piano and said, "Wall, howdy an' a good Christian Sunday mornin' to y'all out thataway." More applause. He said, "I juss figgered I'd lak to invite y'all in fer a reg'lar, good ole-time singin' an' preachin' service lak y'all mebbe used to go to 'way back afore th' fokes in this here country took to gallopin' aroun' almost naked an' usin' drugs an' singin' hippie songs." Still more applause. He said, "I'm talkin' 'bout them there days when a man was head of his own house an' his kids

51

ROSS H. SPENCER

wasn't out in Corvette automobiles peelin' rubber an' runnin' over law-abidin' citizens, back when fokes knowed somethin' about Almighty God an' they pledged allegiance to Ole Glory without gigglin' whilst they done it." He took a drink from the glass on his piano and waited for the applause to dwindle. Then he riffled the piano keys expertly and said, "Now we is down here in Shreveport, Looziana, with all these here fine, God-fearin' Christian fokes an' we is about to kick off this here li'l git-together with a good ole gospel number what my dear ole mother used to sing to me back whilst I was wearin' knee pants." He chuckled and said, "Lawd, have mussy, I must of been a sight to behold! Cain't y'all juss imagine me wearin' knee pants?" The audience tittered into a sea of white handkerchiefs and Huskin said, "My dear ole mother would sit down at that beat-up ole piano my daddy traded up fer a heifer an' two speckled shoats an' she'd say, 'Johnny, honey, y'all come over here an' let me sing y'all a tune 'bout life's railway to Heaven.' With that, Johnny Huskin launched an all-out attack on his piano and tore into "Life's Railway to Heaven." He was backed by an organ, a dobro, a rhythm guitar, a bass fiddle and drums and they really rared back and let fly.

It was infectious music with a lusty, throbbing beat and at the end of the second chorus Johnny Huskin vamped a few bars and hollered, "Awright, now, ever'body! Want y'all to stan' up an' chime right in an' help ole John sing this here song!" The capacity crowd popped obediently to its feet and the rafters were ringing when the television picture faded to a taped commercial and a glib-tongued announcer who explained how one could go about receiving the Johnny Huskin Hallelujah Bible.

The offer was two months old, the announcer said, and this would be its final week of availability. It developed that the Johnny Huskin Hallelujah Bible was bound in saddle-brown genuine calfskin. It was leather-lined with semi-overlapping covers and it featured 23 carat gold-edged India paper with easy-to-read Cameo print. It was a King James version red-letter edition with center references and sixteen colored maps with gazetteer. It was, to put it mildly, the very finest Bible available anywhere and Johnny Huskin would send it postpaid and per-

MONASTERY NIGHTMARE

sonally autographed to the first one thousand people who'd contribute five hundred dollars or more to the Johnny Huskin Evangelistic Association Emergency Plan for the care and feeding of starving children in northern Borneo. The announcer took a deep breath, smiled disarmingly and added that such contributions were, of course, tax deductible.

I turned the television set off. The lay of the land was perfectly obvious. The starving children in northern Borneo would receive a few hundred bucks and the remainder of the bundle would be put down as administrative costs. It would end up in the Chicago Second National Bank and Johnny Huskin would tack a four-room addition onto his already too-large house in White Birch Knolls. I shrugged. With all those sheep standing in line, begging to be sheared, you could hardly blame Huskin. He'd done it all on his own. He'd started from somewhere south of scratch and he'd built a little empire. And, for all I knew, his dear ole mother had really called him to the piano and sang "Life's Railway to Heaven."

I opened another can of Stroh's and sat pondering the stupendous gullibility of the American public. Then, on the spur of the moment, I grabbed the telephone and called Mary O'Rourke's apartment. Mary sounded sleepy. She said, "Good Lord, Luke, it's Sunday morning!"

I said, "What about it?"

"I'm still in bed."

"Alone?"

"Until you get here."

"I have a headache."

"Drinking with Stash Dubinski last night?"

"We had a few."

"You had a few cases. If you'd been with me you wouldn't have a headache. What's on your mind?"

I said, "Mary, somewhere along the line you've mentioned that you know a girl who works at Chicago Second National."

"Mmmmm-m-m, let's see. Oh, yes, Bertha Zane. Why?"

"Is she a teller?"

"No, I believe she works in bookkeeping. Luke, Bertha weighs over two hundred."

"I wonder if she'd do me an off-the-record favor."

53

ROSS H. SPENCER

"I'm sure she would but I'd do it better and I wouldn't care if it was off the record or not."

"I'm not sure we're on the same railroad."

"Neither am I. How'd you like to toot your whistle at the crossing?"

I considered it. I should never consider it. Considering it leads to rash decisions. I said, "Half an hour?"

"Don't bother knocking."

Sometimes my headaches vanish almost instantly.

17

*T*he Pelican Club was a posh, private establishment on the west side of La Salle Street, a stately blend of walnut paneling, rich scarlet carpeting and crystal chandeliers the size of Volkswagens. Wall-to-wall wallop. It cost a grand to join and five hundred a year to stay on the books. The food was excellent, the drinks mellow, the service superb and I wasn't a member. A haughty tuxedo-clad maître d' sized me up. The way you size up an expressway flat tire. He said, "You'll find the employment office to the rear of the building, off the alley."

I said, "I'm to meet Mr. William Westerville."

The maître d' double-clutched smoothly into another gear. He smiled ingratiatingly, bowed and said, "Why, certainly! Please follow me, sir!"

We found Buck Westerville in a high-backed booth in a corner of the immense dining room. On his table were glasses and a tall, frosty pitcher of martinis. I sat across from him and poured for myself. Buck grinned broadly. He said, "I just left Crystal Ball. She wanted your home address."

I said, "And?"

"And I gave it to her."

I said, "I ought to kick your fucking teeth out."

Buck made a deprecatory gesture. "She'd have found you anyway, Luke. All she had to do was tail you home from your office."

I said, "Crystal Ball couldn't tail a green horse on a purple merry-go-round."

Buck dug and dealt out a twenty and a five. He pushed the

ROSS H. SPENCER

bills across the table to me. "I charged her fifty. Split the take and call it square. Luke, how'd you like to make a tall stack of money?"

I slipped the twenty-five bucks into my wallet. "How tall?"

Buck rolled his quick dark eyes. "God knows. Five digits for sure, chance for six."

"For what? Going over Niagara Falls on a surfboard?"

"Low-profile job. You won't even have to go out on the street. Just dust off your typewriter and do a little writing."

I shook my head. "Buck, I'm no writer. I lucked out on one short story back when Christ was a corporal. Any damn fool could have done that."

Buck watched me half smilingly. The way you watch a puppy fall down the stairs. He said, "Luke, this'll be duck soup for you." He leaned toward me and lowered his voice to a confidential level. "I want you to write a Hillary Condor book."

I gave Buck Westerville a long, steady stare. I said, "You talk like a man with a paper ass."

Buck scowled. He said, "Look, Luke, this is the chance of a goddam lifetime! You're a student of Carl Garvey. You know Garvey's style, you know how his stuff is structured, you know his characters inside out. Hell, I'll bet you even know if Miriam Mission has a birthmark."

I said, "Well, now that you mention it, she does. It's an oblong black mole way up high on the inside of her left thigh, almost on the buttock."

Buck slapped the table. "So there, goddammit! Who the hell else would know that?"

I shrugged. I said, "Hillary Condor, for one."

"Luke, Carl Garvey's dead and his last book was something called *One-Way Ticket to Hell*, right?"

"Right."

"Okay, now what if he'd written one more, a manuscript that just blew in out of nowhere? With Garvey's death just a fraction on the questionable side, with his readers missing him and perhaps wondering if he's *really* dead, would that book sell?"

I felt a tingle scoot across the back of my neck. I said, "Of course it'd sell. It'd sell like immortality pills."

MONASTERY NIGHTMARE

Buck licked his lips nervously and the martini pitcher shook in his hand. He said, "How many copies, would you say?"

I pushed it around in my mind. "Well, Garvey was popular. His books sold a couple hundred thousand each. Under these circumstances one more novel might hit a half million."

Buck clenched a white-knuckled fist. He said, "My God, Luke, it'd be a jackpot!"

I said, "Get off that cloud, Buck. You can do time for fraud."

Buck said, "You worry about you and let me worry about me. Could you do a Hillary Condor novel?"

"Possibly, but I won't."

"Luke, they couldn't get within ten miles of you! You'd sign nothing, you'd take your cuts in cash, there'd be no way on earth you could be linked to it!"

I nipped at my martini. There'd been times when I'd felt that I could have out-Garveyed Garvey with his own characters. It was something I'd always had a hankering to try. It would be a kicks project and there'd be money in it. Buck broke in on my thoughts. "How long would it take you to write something like that?"

I said, "The Hillary Condor stuff usually came out at about a hundred and eighty pages. That's maybe two and a quarter in manuscript form, depending on the way they lay it out." I shrugged. "I don't know. Probably not very long if I could come up with a story line."

Buck's dark eyes flashed with excitement. "What an absolute natural! A best-selling author disappears and then his last book hits the stands! Wow!"

"What would be in it for me?"

"Plenty!"

"Give me the bottom line."

Buck didn't hesitate. "Two grand in advance and five percent of the action. At a sawbuck a copy you'd be in line for a couple hundred grand if it'd go half a million in sales."

"It may not be as easy as it seems, Buck. It's going to have to look kosher. Who's supposed to discover this manuscript?"

"Leave that to me, Luke. I got connections."

"So does a guy in an electric chair."

He poured and killed the pitcher of martinis. He said, "Luke,

57

Ross H. Spencer

the less you know about this operation the better off we're going to be. Just take my word for it, the machinery will be greased from here to Manhattan. Give me something that'll pass for Carl Garvey and we're up to our balls in clover!"

"Until somebody blows the whistle."

Buck's smile was scornful. "Who's gonna blow it? Carl Garvey?" Our waiter brought big, leather-bound menus but Buck waved them away. He ordered another pitcher of martinis, T-bone steaks medium well, fries, and salads with vinegar and oil. He glanced at me. The supercilious glance of the provider at the provided-for. He said, "That sound okay? You up to a T-bone?"

I said, "Right about now I'm up to half a brontosaurus. What happens when Garvey's agent reads a book that Garvey didn't write?"

Buck's smile was crafty. "Unlikely and of damned little consequence. I've heard that she's going out of business. Garvey was her bread and butter."

"She?"

"I think so. Is that unusual?"

"Probably not. Just curious. My agent was a woman. What's her name?"

"I'm not sure that I've ever heard it. It isn't important."

"Local woman?"

"Beats me. Don't get hung up on it, Luke. Tell me, can you get right at this?"

There it was—another chance to say no. I let it slip away. I said, "I suppose so. I'm a hunt-and-peck typist. If I can herd it together I'll need somebody who can do a final draft and that could be risky."

Buck stroked his jowl. "Itchy Balzino mentioned that Crystal Ball is one helluva typist. It's an ill wind that bloweth no man to good."

"I can get along without Crystal Ball. Also the Shakespeare quotes."

"That wasn't Shakespeare. It was John Heywood."

The waiter came with our new martini pitcher. He said, "Sir, are you Mr. Luke Lassiter?"

I said, "For what it's worth."

58

MONASTERY NIGHTMARE

The waiter said, "There was a telephone call from a lady named Crystal Ball."

I said, "Was she quoting Shakespeare?"

"No, sir."

"Then you had a different Crystal Ball."

The waiter looked puzzled. He said, "Sir, she said to tell you to buy some licorice."

I glared at Buck Westerville. "How the hell does Crystal Ball know that I'm at the Pelican Club?"

Buck cleared his throat. He said, "I may have mentioned that we'd be having lunch."

I said, "You bastard."

Buck filled our martini glasses. He said, "You know, I just read somewhere that licorice is an aphrodisiac."

18

I went home at dusk, half-looped. I kicked off my shoes and rustled up a Herkimer cheese sandwich and a bottle of Stroh's. Then I parked myself cross-legged in front of my dusty bookcase. My library wouldn't have held much appeal for the intelligentsia. There were a few westerns, two or three shaggy books on the Civil War and a couple of sci-fi stories. There was a *Roget's Thesaurus*, a paperback dictionary and a baseball encyclopedia. The rest was Carl Garvey. Those vividly colored, intriguing dust jackets bore titles like *Murder Wears a Lace Brassiere, Full Moon Over South Hades, Serenade in Blood* and *Death by Ecstasy.* There were twenty-three in all, hard-boiled, wryly humorous tales, seething sex and violence, each with a clever little O'Henry-type twist in its final pages. They certainly didn't amount to literature in the classic sense of the word and it was extremely doubtful that they amounted to literature in *any* sense of the word but they provided hammer-and-tongs entertainment. I hadn't *read* the Carl Garvey novels, I'd *plunged* through them. Traveling with Garvey had been like going to a five-alarm fire on the ass end of a hook-and-ladder unit driven by a drunken fugitive from an insane asylum. It was formula writing, of course, sixty pages to establish a situation, sixty to get Hillary Condor into one Christ-awful jam and sixty more to get him out. I sat skimming the cream from the yellowing old thrillers and found myself on memory lane, recalling clearly where I'd been when I'd read of Hillary Condor's to-the-death struggle with the Phantom Samurai Swordsman high on Mt.

MONASTERY NIGHTMARE

Fuji's frozen slopes or of his seduction of the sinister Cobra Lady from New Delhi.

The hours swept by on silent wings and my eyes grew weary. It was well beyond midnight when I finished leafing through *The Kremlin Is Missing* and returned it to the bookcase. I picked up the empty beer cans, dumped my ashtray and plodded into the bedroom. I was ten thousand years old.

I fell into a troubled sleep to dream a very bad dream.

Just as I'd done when I'd read Carl Garvey a long, long time ago.

19

*I*n my crazy dream a bell was tolling the death knell of civilization. *Ding-dong, ding-dong.* From a very great distance. *Ding-dong*, over and over, and I was thinking that if I could just get to that bell and slug the dirty sonofabitch who was ringing it I might still be able to save the planet from destruction.

Ding-dong. I sat up in bed to look at the clock on my nightstand: 1:25. I'd been in bed less than an hour. *Ding-dong.* Damn! My doorbell! I found my slippers and stumbled into the living room. I opened the door. Crystal Ball sauntered in. She wore a sheer white blouse, navy-blue slacks so tight that they appeared to have been sprayed on and bayonet-heeled white pumps. She said, "Well, hello again."

I said, "Oh, my God."

Crystal Ball said, "There is no woman's sides can bide the beating of so strong a passion as love doth give my heart, no woman's heart so big to hold so much."

I said, "I see." I really didn't.

She said, "Shakespeare."

I said, "Yes." I stared at this willowy, peroxide-blonde damsel of fewer than twenty-five years. She had enormous dark-amber eyes, a Lana Turner nose, a full, ripe, eager mouth, a long-stemmed, taut-bosomed body, a crocheted white handbag with wooden handles and a volume of Shakespeare the size of a small mattress.

That wasn't all.

She had the biggest, blackest Luger pistol I'd ever laid eyes on and she was pointing the damned thing directly at my navel. She

MONASTERY NIGHTMARE

smiled. Sweetly. Her teeth were even and white. She said, "Now you just toddle back into the bedroom and get out of those silly pajamas."

I stared at the Luger and said, "Yes, ma'am."

In view of the circumstances it seemed an appropriate response.

20

It was nearly three in the morning and I'd been kept busy. Hors d'oeuvres are one thing. A twenty-seven-course banquet is an entirely different matter. Crystal Ball had murmured, "Love's tongue proves dainty Bacchus gross in taste."

I'd said, "That's one way of putting it."

She'd gestured urgently with her big black Luger pistol and said, "Come up here." Never argue with an armed female. I'd slithered obediently to her side and she'd rolled to meet me. Very gently she'd pressed the muzzle of the gun to my lips. She'd said, "Open your mouth, lover."

I'd said, "I can't. I think I got lockjaw."

"Come on, baby, open wide for Mommy."

Cold sweat had beaded my forehead. She'd gone canaries! I'd said, "Looky, Crystal, can't we talk this over?"

She'd said, "Open your mouth, damn you!" Her finger had tightened on the trigger. I'd gulped hard and complied. She'd slipped the muzzle of the Luger into my mouth. She'd giggled. She'd said, "Take a big bite. It's licorice."

Now the licorice Luger was nearly gone but its aroma hung heavy in the darkness of my bedroom. Crystal Ball gave me a long, licorice-flavored kiss. She said, "When love speaks, the voice of all the gods make heaven drowsy with the harmony." She bit a chunk out of the Luger's handle and munched audibly. She said, "You are mine, you sonofabitch."

I said, "Well, kiddo, I can take a joke as well as anybody but the next time you pull one like this I'm going to stick your candy

MONASTERY NIGHTMARE

pistol in a place you are going to have a very difficult time getting it out of."

Crystal yawned. She said, "I'll try anything once." She looked at me dreamily. "Fifty bucks for your address but, oh, sweetheart, was it ever *worth* it!"

I said, "Why all the Mickey Mouse? Why didn't you just come up to my office?"

Crystal Ball ran a darting, inquisitive, licorice-stained tongue along my lips. She said, "Your elevator's busted."

21

Crystal sat at the breakfast table with me. In the buff. She said, "How's the coffee?"

I studied the thick, ebony fluid in my cup. I said, "I haven't tried it. It intimidates me."

"I put licorice in it." I swallowed hard. Crystal said, "In New Orleans they put chicory in the coffee."

I sipped at the stuff. It was almost as bad as I'd anticipated. I said, "Uhh-h-h, Crystal, just how long had you planned to stay?"

Crystal peered at me over the rim of her cup. Peek-a-boo style. Her big dark-amber eyes were reproachful. She said, "How long, Luke Lassiter? Did you ask how long, my sweet?"

I said, "Well, yes, I believe that's the way I put it."

Crystal finished her coffee in a gulp and bounced to her feet. She stretched her arms toward the morning sun. My kitchen window faces east, otherwise this would have been very difficult. She said, "How long? How long? This question doth he ask of me!" She clasped her bare breasts so tightly that the flesh bulged between her fingers. She said, "Love's not Time's fool, though rosy lips and cheeks within his bending sickle's compass come."

I said, "I don't believe that quite answers my question."

Crystal continued. I'd been afraid that she might do that. She said, "Love alters not with his brief hours and weeks but bears it out even to the edge of doom."

I said, "Well, speaking of doom, what happens to me when Itchy Balzino comes up here to take you home?"

"Itchy won't do that. Itchy loves me."

"If he loves you he wants you back."

66

MONASTERY NIGHTMARE

"No, Itchy just wants me to be happy. He loves me differently than you do." She poured more licorice coffee. She had a fantastic body.

I said, "I can't recall having said that I love you."

"Oh, but you have. You don't realize it but you have. Love looks not with the eyes but with the mind, and therefore is wing'd Cupid painted blind."

I said, "Well, I was just curious." I put on my hat and Crystal took my arm to escort me to the door. She said, "Do you like Shakespeare?"

I said, "Better than Hemingway."

"Bring home some licorice." She kissed my cheek.

Damned if I didn't like it.

22

*T*here was a neighborhood library a half mile south and I stopped there. I found a copy of *Writer's Market* and paged my way to Authors' Agents. There were three literary agents in all of Chicago, a Richard Bartlett on North Ashland, a J. Mossik and Associates on South Michigan and a Pamela Frost on West Monroe Street. Pamela Frost was the name of the agent who'd arranged my only sale back when the world was young. I'd never met her. I'd never so much as spoken to her. All of our dealings had been carried out by mail.

Her office was on the second floor of an ancient red-brick building on the north side of Monroe a few doors east of La Salle. The elevator was tired and creaky but at least it worked. The sign on the door glass said PAMELA FROST, LITERARY AGENT. THE HELL YOU CAN'T WRITE. Apparently she was a positive thinker. The door squawked like a startled duck when I stepped into a tiny office that was desperately in need of paint. There was an old green metal desk and there was a telephone on it. Nothing else, not a paper clip, not a pencil, not a ballpoint pen. I saw a large, dented metal cabinet on which rested a portable cassette player that emitted the strains of a Scott Joplin tango. The rug was threadbare and the room's only window commanded a magnificent view of an alley strewn with the contents of spilled trash cans. The woman at the desk didn't look up. She said, "Yes?"

I said, "You never can tell." She laughed. It was a light, musical laugh. I said, "You're Pamela Frost?"

She said, "Yes, and you?"

MONASTERY NIGHTMARE

I said, "Luke Lassiter. I'm a private detective. Of a sort, that is."

Pamela Frost smiled. She said, "Then we're well met, Mr. Lassiter. I'm a literary agent, of a sort, that is." I liked her. She was a large woman, red-faced, pushing fifty, heavy-boned, some sixty pounds overweight with an ass like a forty-dollar cow's. She had a prominent high-bridged nose and a wide, thin-lipped mouth. Her hair was ash-blonde and graying, she had thick, masculine hands and she wore little or no makeup. Her dress was simple and navy-blue, the kind designed to make fat women look not so fat, and she wore a pair of large-lensed, metal-trimmed dark glasses. She said, "Sit down, Mr. Lassiter. *Luke* Lassiter, did you say?"

"That's right."

"Well, there's a coincidence. Years ago I sold a short story by a gentleman named Luke Lassiter."

I said, " 'Lilacs Are Fatal.' What happened to the other dozen?"

She extended her hand to me. She had the grip of a lumberjack. She said, "Well, I'll be damned! Pleased to meet you, Luke Lassiter!" She sat, shaking her head in disbelief and saying, "Small world! Small world!"

I said, "When you sold 'Lilacs Are Fatal' I thought I might be off and running."

"You had just one problem, Mr. Lassiter. Your style was so very similar to that of Carl Garvey. Why, gosh, I could have passed your stuff for his. Have you read Carl Garvey?"

"Every word."

"That probably explains it. He may have had a subliminal influence on your writing. I thought you had tons of raw talent."

"Apparently you're familiar with Garvey's stuff."

"Well, my God, yes! I was Carl's literary agent. I'm hopeful that you're investigating some aspect of his tragic death. I've always thought *some*one should dig into the matter."

"I'm not investigating anything, Miss Frost. I've been meaning to drop by for years. You think there's something strange about the Garvey thing?"

Pamela Frost drummed the hard rubber of her desktop with blunt, broad, unpolished fingernails. She said, "Well-l-l, I've

69

Ross H. Spencer

never doubted that Carl was dead. But was his death accidental, was it a heart attack, was he murdered, was it suicide, what the hell happened?"

"Why would you consider murder or suicide?"

"Simply because everything wasn't peaches-and-cream in Carl Garvey's life. His wife was a full-blown little tart. His lawyer borrowed funds from Carl. I use the term loosely."

"Was the money replaced?"

"I believe so, but the point is that Carl was surrounded by piranhas and there's no telling how this may have twisted his thinking. Am I talking too much?"

"No, this is very interesting. My father would have been just as interested in learning the ups and downs of Clarence E. Mulford's life. He read Mulford like I read Garvey."

"Mulford. Let's see . . . Hopalong Cassidy, Red Connors, Johnny Nelson, Buck Peters, Mesquite Jenkins . . . that bunch?"

"You'd have to ask my father. I was all tied up with Hillary Condor. Something I always wondered about: Why did Carl Garvey buy that old monastery on the Fox?"

Pamela Frost smiled pensively. "On a whim. It's worthless. The roof's off and the second floor has caved in but the land is nice. Ideal for picnics and making love."

"You were close with Garvey?"

She thought about it. After a time she said, "How close can you get?"

"Tell me."

"Do you remember when Miriam Mission first appeared in the Hillary Condor series?"

"Sure. Second book. *Murder Wears a Lace Brassiere.*"

Pamela Frost ran her heavy fingers through her graying hair. "Well, Mr. Lassiter, at that time I wore a lace brassiere and Miriam Mission is the Pamela Frost of more than twenty years ago. Miriam looks as I did then, she has my sexual voraciousness and my old get-up-and-go." I whistled and Pamela Frost smiled her toothy smile. She said, "You *should* whistle! I haven't always been fifty and overweight!"

I didn't touch it but I felt sorry for this big, open woman. Her tape player had been doing the same tango, again and again. I said, "Your favorite song?"

70

MONASTERY NIGHTMARE

"One of them. Tangos turn me on. May I call you Luke?"

"Be my guest. What turns you off?"

"Nothing short of enough." There was that stare and the odd smile.

I said, "Dinner some evening?"

"I thought you'd never ask. I enjoy talking to you." She fidgeted on her chair. "I think very young, Luke." There was a sadness about her. "You might be surprised *how* young."

She was laying it right on the line but I didn't get a feeling of brazenness. She gave the impression of being downright clinical. Well, if I was going to do a Garvey-style book it wouldn't hurt to know more about Garvey. I stood and said, "So long, Miss Frost."

She said, "Pam."

"Pam." I waved and went out. On Monroe Street I whistled a few bars of Pamela Frost's tango. When she hadn't returned my wave I knew why Buck Westerville had said it was unlikely that she'd be reading a new Carl Garvey novel.

I wondered how long she'd been blind.

23

*I*n my office I checked my answering device and found the tape to be blank. That was good. I was in a mood to get at Hillary Condor. I sharpened a few pencils and dug a legal pad from a desk drawer. Then I sat there, trying to think like Carl Garvey had thought, staring at the yellow paper, doodling, waiting for an idea. Half a dozen Marlboros later one came hobbling along and I threw a hammerlock on it. Why not write a story about a man who'd gone sailing, never to return? But this man wouldn't be Carl Garvey. He'd be a brilliant young physicist with a revolutionary nuclear formula. I'd call him Professor James. Professor James would be desperately afraid that his formula would fall into the wrong hands so, to protect it, he'd concoct a secret code, bury the formula in a mishmash of numerals and burn the original.

Okay, then what?

I knocked it around for a few minutes and then I remembered that Carl Garvey had bought the old monastery on the Fox river. I'd use that monastery. I'd have a pair of aging monks holed up in it. They'd be Brother Sigfried and Brother Luigi. While on a fishing trip Professor James would meet these monks and, greatly impressed by their dedication, he'd entrust his coded formula to them with the request that it be safeguarded until such time as it could be adapted to the benefit of mankind rather than to the certain annihilation of same. The monks would throw Professor James a few *pax vobiscums* or whatever monks say under such circumstances and Professor James would go sailing to vanish from the face of the earth, never once sus-

MONASTERY NIGHTMARE

pecting that Brother Sigfried is nuttier than a carload of Georgia fruitcakes or that Brother Luigi is no great bargain either. Brother Sigfried would be an ex–SS officer with a wealth of experience in cryptography and Brother Luigi would be a bastard son of Benito Mussolini and both would be on the lam from a whole mess of war-crimes charges. They'd haul out the midnight oil and before you could say *Deutschland über alles* they'd crack the flimsy code of Professor James. Then they'd set about the naughty business of constructing a nuclear bomb capable of blowing up the fucking universe.

The ingredients for this hellish device would be scrounged up with the satanic assistance of a witch's coven that meets in the woods behind the monastery at midnight on the third Thursday of each month. Everything would be just hunky-dory and it would appear that the Fourth Reich is just around the corner when Hillary Condor would get wind of the deal. Hillary would drag Miriam Mission's divine keester out of the sack and they'd hop into Condor's jet-black helicopter and haul-ass for the scene of activity. Now the manure would really hit the windmill and it'd be Katy-bar-the-door with naked broads cantering in every conceivable direction and dead bodies strewn from horizon to horizon.

I figured I'd call it *Monastery Nightmare* and I lit into the project with great gusto. By four that afternoon I'd done more than twenty pages. Then I settled back and read it through, made corrections, added a few Garvey-style clichés and called Crystal Ball. I said, "Would you be up to doing some typing this evening?"

Crystal said, "I would if I had a typewriter."

"I'll bring my office portable. Run down to the drugstore and get a few tablets of typing paper."

"Oh, darn! I just came from there. I was looking for licorice."

"Find any?"

"Not a bit."

I grabbed my old L. C. Smith and headed for the Adams Street parking lot. On my way I stopped at a candy store and spent twenty-five dollars for a thirty-pound licorice antiaircraft gun. I could hardly get the damned thing into my car.

24

The Lassiters keep their promises and I was keeping mine in spite of my misgivings. Barbara Huskin had picked me up at Bessie Barnum's Circus Tap and we were in her powder-blue Mercedes headed for the Blotters Club meeting at Elizabeth Fudge's place. I said, "Barb, who are we chasing?"

"Nobody. Why?"

"Okay, then who's chasing us?"

"I get it. I'm driving too fast."

"Well, you're in no danger of getting arrested for loitering."

"Luke, we have to be at Elizabeth's in less than ten minutes. Elizabeth runs a tight ship and her meetings begin precisely on time." The Fudge residence stood on the west side of Plum Street at the north end of Elmwood Park. It was a vintage structure, gaunt and gray, and as we pulled into the driveway Barb said, "This house reminds me so much of Elizabeth. Isn't that funny?"

I said, "Not if you're Elizabeth."

"Oh, I meant nothing derogatory by the remark, Luke, but it's odd how so many houses come to mirror their owners." We pulled into the driveway, got out, and Barb guided me toward the rear entrance. We passed a small brown Plymouth that bulged with atlases, encyclopedias, books of quotations, almanacs and concordances. Barb said, "We refer to this as the Swisher Mobile Research Library."

I said, "How can she see to drive?"

Barb said, "She leaves a peephole between *Bartlett's Familiar Quotations* and *Webster's Dictionary of Synonyms*." Elizabeth

MONASTERY NIGHTMARE

Fudge met us at the door. She was gaunt and gray with the shape of a praying mantis and the facial characteristics of a Boy Scout hatchet that has been used to sever steel girders. She wore thick-lensed, rimless glasses and a hearing aid half the size of a 1936 Atwater-Kent table model radio. She smiled at Barb and frowned at me. Simultaneously. Barb said, "Elizabeth, this is Mr. Luke Lassiter."

Elizabeth Fudge studied me the way you study a fly in your chicken salad sandwich. She put out her hand as though she was about to plunge it into a steaming mound of dragon dung. She said, "You are a private investigator, Mr. Lassiter?"

I said, "I'm so private hardly anybody knows I'm in business."

Barb cut in. She said, "Oh, Elizabeth, he's very, very good!" Elizabeth Fudge cleared her throat, too loudly and too long, I thought. Barb said, "In his chosen field of endeavor, that is." Her face was the color of a Martian sunset. She mumbled, "Or so I've been given to understand."

Fudge stared thoughtfully at Barb. She said, "Well, Mr. Lassiter, you'll find fruit punch on the kitchen table. The bathroom's just down the hall across from Edgar's den. We have barely two minutes until meeting time." She scurried into the living room, Barb headed for the bathroom and I was alone in the kitchen. I took the pint of 190 proof grain alcohol from my jacket pocket and emptied the bottle into Elizabeth Fudge's big bowl of fruit punch. I stirred deftly with a forefinger. 190 proof grain alcohol is very easily disguised. I'd learned that in the army.

I drifted into Fudge's nineteenth-century parlor and met Geraldine Swisher and Candy Stoneman. Geraldine was a tubby, brown-haired little woman in her sixties. She was seated in a Morris chair and she nodded to me almost imperceptibly. She had a ruddy complexion, dark blue eyes and one of those don't-push-me jaws. She wore a black business suit, a white ruffled blouse and high brown boots of excellent leather. Candy Stoneman was something else. She was in her late twenties, blonde and assembled like a half-million-dollar thoroughbred filly. She had flashing gray eyes, a full-lipped mouth, dazzling white teeth and an awe-inspiring bosom. Her purple blouse was sheer, her orange skirt was short and flimsy, her long legs were

ROSS H. SPENCER

crossed and I saw no signs of a half-slip. She was one of those chickies who believe that if you have it there's nothing to be gained by keeping it a secret. She met my gaze unblinkingly and said, "We're so pleased to have you with us tonight, Mr. Lassiter. Elizabeth has been considering bringing in a private detective for some time now." She uncrossed and recrossed her legs. I'd been right the first time. No half-slip. Her panties were black. She said, "How did Barbara come to select you?"

I said, "She probably threw darts at a bankruptcy list."

Geraldine Swisher stirred in her Morris chair and said, "Research reveals that there are fewer than five hundred bona fide private investigators in the Chicago metropolitan area. The ratio to citizens is utterly disproportionate, amounting to less than one in ten thousand."

On a stool in front of an old upright piano Elizabeth Fudge squirmed nervously, checking her watch every five seconds. When Barb came into the room she waved to Geraldine and Candy and sat beside me on the davenport. She put her mouth to my ear and said, "I just did something nice for you. I dumped a pint of 190 proof grain alcohol into Elizabeth's fruit punch."

I said, "Oh, Jesus Christ!"

Elizabeth Fudge glared at me from her piano stool. She said, "Is something wrong, Mr. Lassiter?"

I said, "Not yet."

Barb whispered, "Don't worry, they'll never taste it. 190 proof grain alcohol is very easily disguised."

I whispered, "Who told you that?"

Barb whispered, "My father. He learned it in the army."

The big moment was upon us. Elizabeth Fudge was waving for attention in the fashion of a British sentinel signaling an all-out Zulu charge. She peered at her wristwatch. She said, "Blotters, are we ready?" Apparently the Blotters were ready. Fudge said, "All right, ladies, this is it!" She raised her hands above her head and led the Blotters Club in the Blotters Club cheer:

MONASTERY NIGHTMARE

WRITE, GIRLS, WRITE!
WRITE, GIRLS, WRITE!
WRITE, GIRLS!
WRITE, GIRLS!
WRITE, GIRLS, WRITE!

There was applause and Elizabeth Fudge beamed with pleasure. She said, "Thank you, Blotters! As you know, the Blotters Club cheer is a short composition of mine." She grinned. I think it was a grin. With Elizabeth Fudge I couldn't be certain. I have the same difficulty with alligators. She said, "Oh, girls, pure genius is so capricious, is it not?"

I stared at Barb. Barb kicked my ankle.

Elizabeth Fudge's bony hands hovered above the old piano's keys. Like birds of prey above a flock of defenseless lambs. She said, "And now for the Blotters Club Song, which I wrote, of course." Her fingers plunged to the keyboard and I winced as the ancient upright bleated in discordant agony. The words of the Blotters Club Song had been set to the melody of "Flow Gently, Sweet Afton." I think.

> *Write swiftly, ye-ee Blotters,*
> *Write swiftly, I say,*
> *And you will be famous as I am someday.*
> *Write swiftly, ye-ee Blotters,*
> *And harken to me!*
> *We won't waste our talents on porn-og-raph-ee.*

I lunged blindly into the kitchen and stopped short. The level of Elizabeth Fudge's punch bowl had receded and at the kitchen table I saw a short, fat guy wearing a bed sheet and a white skull cap. He gazed at me with kindly, long-suffering eyes. He smiled and placed a pudgy hand on my forearm. He said, "My blessings go with thee, my son."

I knelt and said, "Thank you, Holy Father." We filled our glasses from the punch bowl and toasted each other silently. Then he tottered aimlessly down the hall and I returned to the living room where Elizabeth Fudge was saying, "Blotters, in order that we may have more time to visit with our guest of the

ROSS H. SPENCER

evening, we will eliminate our customary session of pin-the-tail-on-the-donkey. Please help yourselves to the fruit punch and get back as rapidly as possible."

They filed into the kitchen and Barb was the first to return. She was smacking her lips. She said, "Luke, it's nothing short of delicious. I don't detect the alcohol."

I nodded. I said, "Custer didn't detect the Indians."

25

*T*he antique clock on Elizabeth Fudge's mantel had just bonged eleven times and the punch bowl was running perilously low. Barbara Huskin sat beside me on the davenport, her head in her hands. Candy Stoneman watched me with bloodshot eyes. She looked puzzled and she kept shaking her head like there was water in her ears. Elizabeth Fudge stared at me through thick lenses and said, "I simple muss get this preschipmunk change. There seven too manys of you."

Geraldine Swisher steadied herself in the Morris chair. She said, "Sho ish then wash happening when KGB agensh try excape?"

I said, "Well, by that time there were only twenty-five of 'em so I just cut 'em down with my Browning automatic rifle."

Geraldine Swisher said, "Eggzhackle what I would do under circular simmenstances."

Elizabeth Fudge nodded sagely. She said, "Hereby make moshun no KGB agensh allowed in Blotters Club. All in favor shay hi."

Candy Stoneman blinked several times. She said, "This fucking room keeps turning fucking upside fucking down."

Geraldine said, "Wash thish country need ish more patrioks like Mishel Asshitter."

Elizabeth said, "Hereby make moshun we hole big patriok's parade in backyard."

Geraldine said, "Eggshellnut sujjeshun but we doan gonno drum."

Elizabeth said, "Got big washtub in shellar go boom-boom."

ROSS H. SPENCER

Candy Stoneman said, "Some summbish better turn this fucking room off."

Elizabeth said, "Who goan be drummer?"

Geraldine said, "Masher Litslitter be drummer. Need patriok for drummer."

Candy Stoneman got sick on Elizabeth Fudge's 19th-century parlor floor.

We assembled in the kitchen, Elizabeth Fudge in front with an umbrella for a baton. She said, "Forrerd Marsh!" I gave the washtub a whack and we went stomping into the backyard as the strains of Gounod's "Ave Maria" swelled in great volume from the gaunt, gray house on Plum Street.

26

*T*he big, rosy-cheeked, redheaded cop at the desk of the Elmwood Park Police Station was named Kevin O'Shaughnessy. He shuffled disgruntledly through the reports of the arresting officers and said, "Well, lock 'em up, get 'em some black coffee and gimme a chance to get these charges straightened out." He said, "Now, let's see. So far we got 'em on being drunk and disorderly, disturbing the peace and holding a goddam parade without a permit. Jesus Christ, what a mess!"

One of the cops said, "You ain't kiddin'! You seen the backseat of the squad car?"

Sergeant O'Shaughnessy said, "What about the backseat of the squad car?"

The cop said, "The blonde broad got sick all over it."

Sergeant O'Shaughnessy made a note on one of the reports. He mumbled, "Getting sick all over backseat of squad car." The telephone rang and O'Shaughnessy grabbed it. He said, "Elmwood Park Police." He listened for a moment. He said, "Look, turn that goddam organ down, I can hardly hear you." He frowned and said, "Whaddaya mean 'Profanum vulgus' . . . ?" Then he said, "Whaddaya mean 'Quam parva sapiene mundus requitur'? Speak American, for Christ's sake!" In a moment he said, "That's better! . . . From *where*? . . . Sorry, that's out of our jurisdiction." Suddenly O'Shaughnessy's eyes bulged. He said, "The *who*?" The color had faded from his cheeks. He said, "Yes, sir! . . . At *once*, sir!"

Sergeant O'Shaughnessy stood up. He tore up the arrest reports. He pointed a trembling finger at our police escort. He

81

ROSS H. SPENCER

said, "Now, if you bastards don't want to do about five million goddam years in Purgatory you better drive these taxpayers home immediately!" He sagged into his chair and clapped his hands to his head. He said, "Holy Christ, that was the *Vatican!*"

27

Monastery Nightmare rolled better than anything I'd ever attempted to write. Carl Garvey had blazed the trail for me, the guidelines were there, character mannerisms had been firmly established and it was like painting by numbers. By precedent it was essential that a Hillary Condor plot run second to violence and sex and I was a pretty fair hand at grinding out both. In one scene I had Condor decapitate a giant Oriental assassin with a broken butter knife. In another I arranged for him to seduce six movie starlets simultaneously. My only serious hang-up was the monastery. To the best of my recollection I'd never seen such a facility in any state of repair, even in a picture book, and I knew that I'd have to locate Carl Garvey's Fox river property before I'd be capable of describing one with any degree of accuracy.

I was deeply immersed in the story and I'd come to detest interruptions but they came, welcome or not. I had a call from a distraught woman who said, "Oh, my God, Herman is missing!"

I said, "Sorry to hear that."

"Can you find him?"

"Possibly. What does he look like?"

"He's eighteen feet long and he has beautiful splotches."

"I see."

"He's an Indian rock python."

I said, "Well, ma'am, as a matter of fact, at this particular time I'm confronted by several difficult assignments, one of which is the quelling of a Seminole uprising in Alaska."

"The Seminoles are from Florida."

I said, "Yes, but these Seminoles have been drinking."

Ross H. Spencer

She hung up and I went down the hall to the washroom. When I returned to my desk Kenny Blossom was leaning over it, staring at my legal pad. He said, "Hiya, Luke. Your elevator's screwed up."

"I know it."

"What's new, Luke?"

I said, "Well, for one thing there's a fat bastard in my office reading my personal papers."

Kenny said, "What the hell is this crap? Who's Hillary Condor?"

"A stepbrother of Daniel Boone and founder of the Seventh Day Adventist Church. Get away from my goddam desk."

"Hillary Condor. Seems I've heard that name somewhere. I didn't know you wrote things, Luke."

"I don't. I just mess around. Way to kill time."

"I like that title, *Monastery Nightmare*. You think it up all by yourself?"

"Kenny, I'm busy. What's on your mind?"

"I brought up your mail."

"My mailbox is locked."

"Yeah, but this one was sort of sticking out. Just trying to be helpful." He tossed an envelope onto my desk and I glanced at it. In its upper left-hand corner I saw a red rose twined around a cross and, in script, the words JOHNNY HUSKIN EVANGELIS-TIC ASSOCIATION. Probably a check for my services. Some services, Johnny. You could use a few more like me. I dropped the envelope into my desk drawer.

Kenny Blossom said, "Hey, ain't that Johnny Huskin one of them big television preachers?"

I shrugged and managed a yawn. I said, "Never heard of him."

"Yeah, he's on every Sunday morning. Always begging for money. You might have something he wants."

I looked Kenny Blossom square in the eyes. I said, "Like *what*?"

Kenny shifted his attention to the lighting of a crooked Italian cigar. He said, "Jeez, Luke, you better get some rest. You're crabby."

"You didn't answer my question."

MONASTERY NIGHTMARE

Kenny looked at me with wide, innocent, watery-blue eyes. He said, "Like money, Luke. What else?" He went out.

Half an hour later Johnny Huskin came in. He wore a tan business suit and oxblood military-style oxfords. His shirt was stiff-collared and snowy-white. His dark-brown necktie carried a white silk-stitched JH and it was adorned with his golden circle of little crosses. There was a red rose in the buttonhole of his left lapel and he was turning his snap-brimmed brown hat self-consciously in his hands. He said, "Lassiter, did y'all know your elevator ain't workin'?"

"Yes, Reverend, it's been out of whack for a couple of weeks."

"Y'all reckon a body could mebbe siddown an' rest his bones a spell?"

I pushed the manuscript to one side and said, "Why not? There ain't nobody here but us chickens."

Huskin sat on the wooden chair, crossed his legs and balanced his hat on his knee. He said, "Thass a country line. Y'all country?"

"Once upon a time. Hubbard, Ohio."

"Ohio. I think we got us a revival booked over thataway after th' first of th' year. Youngstown. Know where Youngstown is?"

"Seven miles from Hubbard."

Huskin said, "Y'all git my check?"

"In today's mail. I haven't looked at it."

"It's all there."

"I'm sure it is. Thanks, Reverend."

"Y'all earned it, Lassiter."

I didn't say anything.

"Sho' wish y'all could drop in on one of our meetin's sometime. A country boy might take a shine to it."

"I thought that your local telecasts were done in the studio."

"Wall, thass mostly true. Recently we been showin' tapes of our Southland Crusade. We juss run Shreveport an' next it's gonna be Jackson but we holds a occasional live Chicago session. I'll let y'all know when."

"Do that, if you will."

"Sho' 'nuff. Wall, Lassiter, I was juss passin' by." He got up and put on his hat. He said, "May Th' Good Lord bless an' keep y'all." He waved and closed the door gently behind him, leaving

85

ROSS H. SPENCER

me to stare into my cracked mirror at Luke Lassiter, the guy who took another man's wife to bed and accepted money for a job he hadn't done. I found Huskin's envelope in my drawer and opened it. Like the envelope the check had a red rose twined around a cross. Pay to the order of Lassiter Private Investigations $1,000.00. One Thousand and 00/100 Dollars. John J. Huskin.

I crossed my forearms on the desk and rested my chin on them.

Christ.

28

I got back to *Monastery Nightmare* but not for long. The telephone broke in on a scene that featured Hillary Condor in a knock-down-drag-out brawl with a pack of rabid Mongolian wolves. Barbara Huskin said, "My God, who are you mad at?"

"Nobody. Why?"

"You nearly took my head off."

"Sorry, Barb. I've had a few interruptions this afternoon. Shyster detectives and Indian rock pythons and the like."

"I can call back, Luke. I'm at the pharmacy and I have a bit of shopping to do."

"No, that's okay. What's up?"

"I talked to Elizabeth Fudge this morning and she's fit to be tied!"

"Elizabeth Fudge was probably *born* fit to be tied."

"Yes, but I've never known her to be in a state like this! She asked me to contact you. Luke, Elizabeth has lost her religion!"

"Well, I can't find it for her."

"No, but she has a job for you."

"Beating another washtub?"

"Let me start from the beginning. Elizabeth bitterly resents having been taken into custody by the Elmwood Park Police. She believes she'll carry a criminal's brand to her grave and she feels honor-bound to visit stern retaliation on the community that has treated her so unfairly."

"What's she all stoked up about? The cops tore up the arrest papers. They don't even know her name."

"Luke, she's implacable. Elizabeth wants to commit a *crime!*"

87

Ross H. Spencer

"You mean *How to Be a Christian Although Happily Married* wasn't enough?"

"She's authorized me to offer you five hundred dollars to mastermind a caper for the Blotters Club. It must take place in Elmwood Park."

I said, "Hold it right there. I couldn't mastermind a leopard into a meat market. When I was a kid I swiped some pencils from a guy. He chased me five blocks and when he caught me he kicked my ass into the next county. The sonofabitch wasn't blind in the first place. That's the sort of capers I mastermind."

Barb sounded disappointed. She said, "I thought it might be fun. You see, it doesn't have to be for real."

"Play that one again."

"Well, Elizabeth wants to go first class. She's so furious that she'd be willing to blow the Elmwood Park Police Station to smithereens but she'll settle for a simple robbery. It could be something that she's been led to believe is valuable while, in reality, it's utterly worthless. Do you see what I'm driving at?"

"Are the other girls in on this?"

"Yes, I called them early this afternoon. You make five hundred dollars, Elizabeth gets her revenge and the Blotters Club returns to normal."

I thought about it and grinned. I had the basic ingredients for a lulu but the plan would call for some tall powers of persuasion on my part. I said, "How's about something out of a museum?"

"Great! Just so Elizabeth is convinced that she's stolen something important. Will you work on it?"

"Yeah. Barb, gotta hang up. There's somebody here."

There was somebody there, all right. He stood about six-six and he weighed close to 270. He wore a gray sharkskin suit, black shirt and white tie. He had the shoulders of a grizzly bear and hands like waffle irons. He'd been down the road a piece. His face was a mask of scars, his nose had been bent every way but straight and one ear was twice as thick as the other. He had beady, mean, little brown eyes and he was the sort of character you aren't anxious to meet in dark alleys. He spoke from one corner of a gashlike mouth and his voice had the melodious qualities of a chain saw biting into petrified wood. He scratched the back of his neck and said, "You Luke Lassiter?"

MONASTERY NIGHTMARE

I said, "Yes, sir." I stood up.

He said, "Sit down." I sat down. The customer is always right but some are more right than others. He settled into my wooden chair and scratched his knee. He said, "Lassiter, sweetest little lady which is on earth has move in with some dummy when she's move out on me."

I said, "And you want to know where she is."

He scratched his chest. He said, "She already where I know is this dummy she's move in with."

I said, "I see. Then what can I do for you?"

He scratched his chin and reached to take me by the shoulder. He squeezed and it was like getting caught in a hydraulic press. He said, "You can be real nice on Crystal or I'm kill your ass."

I said, "Look, Mr. Balzino, I don't want any trouble."

Itchy Balzino scratched his ankle. He said, "Trouble? In Newcastle they got coals up the fanny. You got Crystal."

I said. "Do you want her back?"

He scratched his head. He said, "Hey, kid, you crazy?"

I said, "Probably. I let her move in, didn't I?"

Itchy Balzino leaned in my direction, his great shoulders bulging, his beady eyes glittering. He scratched his nose. He said, "Hey, is not making no smart talk on Crystal, a very good girl which she is has always being."

I said, "Helluva typist!"

Itchy said, "Just got couple weaknesses like which is everybody else of us got also too."

I said, "Licorice and Shakespeare."

Itchy scratched his elbow. He said, "The licorice okay but that Shakespeare no speak English."

I said, "He's dead, Mr. Balzino."

He scratched his navel and shrugged. He said, "Well, we all gotsa go sometime."

I said, "How long was Crystal your girl friend, Mr. Balzino?"

Itchy Balzino stood up. He grabbed me by the front of my shirt. He lifted me from my chair and drew me up to where I could smell the Chianti on his breath. He hissed, "*Girl friend?* Why, you wise *bastardo*, you living with my only *figlia!*"

I gulped and croaked, "What's a *figlia?*"

"*Daughter*, dummy!"

89

I said, "But the *name's* different."

"Crystal's knocka offa *zino*." He dropped me into my chair the way you discard a used Kleenex. He said, "Hey, kid, you Catholic?"

I said, "No, sir, but my cousin is."

He nodded thoughtfully. "So long, Lassiter. Parting such sweet sorrow. Crystal always say that. Shakespeare." He went out, scratching his fanny.

I locked up and went down the stairs.

Well, there was always tomorrow. Sometimes I worried about that.

29

*B*uck Westerville's perky little redheaded secretary–receptionist leaped from her chair and waved her arms frantically. I said, "Better level off at five thousand, honey, it gets mighty cold up there."

She said, "But, sir, you can't go in until I've asked Mr. Westerville!"

I said, "It'll be okay." I kicked the office door open. Buck was seated at his desk, studying a typed sheet of paper. Probably a contract selling his mother into slavery. He looked up and plunged a hand into a pants pocket. By the time I reached his desk he was waving a fifty-dollar bill, a green flag of truce. He said, "Now, take it easy, Luke. It was easy money and I've learned not to turn it down."

I said, "Judas Iscariot must have written a book."

"Nobody got hurt, Luke."

"No, but that gorilla could have plucked me like a chicken."

"Itchy wasn't sore. He just wanted to find out if you're Catholic."

"You never told me that Crystal was his daughter. I thought she was his broad."

"Huh-uh, she's *your* broad."

"Crystal's no broad. She's a sweet, mixed-up kid who thinks she's in love with an antique."

Buck gave me a slow, tongue-in-cheek nod. "How's the book coming along?"

"It'd come along a helluva lot better if you'd stop passing out

91

my name and address to the whole goddam world! Once more, Buck, and I'm taking a month's vacation!"

"Aw, c'mon, Luke. Don't get all pissed off."

I said, "Well, what did you expect, the *croix de guerre*?" I folded the fifty-dollar bill and shoved it into my pocket. When I passed the redhead at the desk I said, "Buck told me that it was very thoughtful of me to drop in."

She said, "Kiss my ass."

All factors considered, it's a rotten world.

30

I'd been very diplomatic in my approach to Stash Dubinski. Now, in a dim corner of Bessie Barnum's Circus Tap, Stash stared across the table at me. The way you'd stare at a giant squid in your bathtub. He spoke in awed tones. He said, "Good God, Luke, you just gotta be nuts!"

I said, "Look, Stash, damn near anything would serve the purpose. Just some beat-up old papers, like maybe the inventory report from five years ago. Something that *looks* important but *isn't*. All you gotta do is leave a door unlocked so she can get in, grab whatever it is and haul-ass."

Stash watched me with narrowed eyes. He said, "What's your incentive?"

I said, "A couple hundred bucks. You get half. That comes out to two weeks' free beer." No reason Stash should know *every*thing.

He shook his head. "Luke, you don't know what you're asking! The slightest slip and I'd be looking for a new job!"

"Stash, it couldn't come to that. Three of the four gals are hep to the fact that it'll be a dry run. Nothing to it. Let this old battle-ax steal something worthless and that's the ball game."

"It'll be the ball game if she gets caught. It'll be the fucking *World Series!*"

Stash clammed up when Bessie Barnum brought more beer. Bessie eyed us suspiciously. She said, "You bastards act like you're plotting to overthrow the government."

I said, "Yeah, but first we gotta steal a hydrogen bomb."

Bessie said, "That wouldn't surprise me a bit. I remember

ROSS H. SPENCER

some of your tomfoolery. Like when you kept sneaking gas into Bobo Burke's car and he was going around telling people he was getting four hundred miles to the gallon." She picked up her money and returned to the bar, her shoulders jiggling with silent laughter.

I said, "She's right, Stash. We used to have a lotta fun. Remember when Jake Netherby passed out at the bar and we drove him down to the funeral home and they goddam near embalmed him?"

A slow smile creased Stash Dubinski's rugged countenance. He said, "Yeah, and how about the night we swiped the engine out of Larry Naylor's pickup truck? Boy, were you ever drunk!"

I said, "Maybe I wasn't as drunk as you. That was the transmission."

Stash said, "Well, whatever it was it was heavy." His eyes had grown dreamy and he began to whistle tunelessly. Suddenly his smile burst into full bloom. He popped the table with the flat of his big hairy hand and our glasses danced a gleeful jig. He said, "Luke, this could be just like them days of yore!"

I said, "Why, sure it could, Stash!"

Stash threw back his head and roared with laughter. He said, "Why, we'll fool the bloomers right off this old broad!"

Bessie Barnum was back in our vicinity, wiping a table. She came over to us, frowning. She said, "You'll fool the bloomers right off of *what* old broad?"

I said, "We weren't talking about you, Bessie."

Bessie ignored me. She put her hand on Stash Dubinski's arm. She looked into his eyes. She said, "Honey, anytime you want this old broad's bloomers off all you got to do is ask!"

31

We were on our dozenth beer and Stash Dubinski had just sketched a rough diagram on a paper napkin. He pointed with his ballpoint pen to an opening at one side of his drawing. He said, "This is the door to the furnace room under Leffingwell's south wing. The old magpie will have ten minutes between Rudy Garson going off and Clint Kelly coming on."

"You're absolutely sure of that?"

"Can't miss. Clint Kelly always gets blocked by the train to Barrington at the Des Plaines Northwestern crossing and that makes him five minutes late. Rudy Garson leaves Leffingwell five minutes early so he won't get held up on Grand Avenue by that Milwaukee Road train to Elgin. It's worked to the split second for the last few years."

"You're Leffingwell's security chief. How come you go along with that kind of gap?"

"Well, Clint and Rudy work the south wing and there ain't never been nothing in there until now. Now it's got Rabies Razzano's getaway car and William Tell's bow and arrows and who'd want any of that old junk? Besides, those jobs don't pay worth a damn and guards are hard to come by."

"None of that stuff is being exhibited yet?"

"Not till September. We're working on it. We just put a battery in Razzano's Packard and it'll run but the hand-throttle's rusted wide-open and the brakes are shot."

"Why bother? Nobody's going to drive the damn thing."

"We won't take it on the road but it'll have to be moved from time to time and why push it?"

ROSS H. SPENCER

I said, "Okay, Stash, how does this big heist work?"

Stash grinned conspiratorially and hunched forward over his drawing. His ballpoint pen began to leave light trails on the napkin. He said, "I'll forget to lock the furnace room door and she'll go up these stairs and down this hall to the big room at the end. Over in the right-hand corner behind Razzano's car there's an old desk that the maintenance crew uses and in the top drawer there'll be a wad of papers in a big brown envelope. I'll have it sealed with blue wax and it'll be marked ALLIED FORCES NORMANDY INVASION PLANS MAY 1944 DWIGHT D. EISENHOWER COMMANDING."

"The invasion took place in June."

"Yeah, but it was scheduled for May before the weather turned sour. It won't matter, Luke. These broads probably think Normandy is some kind of perfume."

I said, "Well, just so the envelope looks real important."

Stash chuckled. He said, "Hey, it'll get by! I'm gonna draw a big spread eagle on it and everything! Actually it'll be full of rejected contractor's bids for the new roof and gutters we'll be putting on Leffingwell shortly. By the way, I got that job for my cousin's outfit, Neurotkowski Roofing."

"I've met your cousin. Lennie, isn't it?"

"Yeah, mighty shrewd operator. They thought Shylock was a tightwad until Lennie came along. Now, if this old bat gets home and opens the envelope you just tell her that the invasion plans are in code and that's the reason they look like roofing and gutter estimates. If she gets the lead out she can pull the job and be clear of the neighborhood with three or four minutes to spare."

"Sounds great, Stash. I'll wait in the car with the other three and we'll grab Elizabeth and blow the area in a hurry."

Stash dusted his hands and returned his ballpoint pen to his pocket. He said, "Okay, Luke, so much for that. Now I can get back to worrying about them Red Sea Documents."

"Where you keeping them?"

Stash Dubinski smiled a secret little smile. He leaned forward and lowered his voice a couple of notches. "Until we get the display case ready I got 'em where no sonofabitch would ever

Monastery Nightmare

think of looking. I shoved 'em under the front seat of Rabies Razzano's Packard."

I whistled. "Well, by God, Stash, there's a cute wrinkle!"

Stash said, "Damn tootin', Luke! Hey, I ain't Leffingwell's Chief of Security just on account of I got big feet!"

32

*T*he Kane County Courthouse is located in Geneva, Illinois. Geneva is a hilly picturesque little town on the Fox river. The Fox makes the Ganges look like a crystal mountain brook and the Kane County Courthouse is a cavernous anachronism probably designed by Count Dracula. I didn't fare too well in the early going. I ricocheted from Divorces to Birth Records to Marriage Licenses before I found Real Estate Titles. There a pudgy, sweating, middle-aged clerk peered at me through pop-bottle lenses. He stood motionless, watching me warily, waiting for me to do something terrible. I told him I was interested in locating a Kane County property owned by Mr. Carl Garvey and that rang his bell. He said, "Carl Garvey, the writer?"

"Yes, the writer."

"You ever read any of his stuff?"

"All of it."

"Wasn't he something?"

"Sure was. Where's the property?"

The clerk gave me a meaningful leer. He said, "Man, if I could get my hooks into that Miriam Mission just one damn time she'd throw rocks at Hillary Condor."

I nodded. I'd felt the same way myself in the dear, dead days beyond recall. I said, "How do I find the property?"

The clerk said, "You ever read *The Kremlin Is Missing*?"

"Twice."

"Wasn't that weird, that part in *The Kremlin Is Missing*?"

"Which weird part was that?"

98

MONASTERY NIGHTMARE

"The weird part where Hillary Condor seduces the Commissar's wife in that funeral parlor and takes her to bed in a coffin."

"Yes, now about this property of Garvey's."

"Come to think of it, there was a whole bunch of weird parts in *The Kremlin Is Missing.*"

"I read it."

"What was your favorite weird part?"

"Oh, I don't know. I figure if you've read one weird part you've read them all."

"Hey, how about that weird part where Hillary Condor is climbing the Empire State Building and when he's halfway up he meets that big, hairy-assed gorilla coming down?" He squinted. "Or do I got that weird part mixed up with some other weird part?"

I said, "Looky, why don't you just tell me about Carl Garvey's property?"

"Yeah, the property. I been up to see it, you know."

"No, I wasn't informed."

"Oh, sure. Back in April. That was just so's I could say I been up to see it."

"Right. A man wouldn't want to lie about having been up to see it."

"You can't see much from the road. It ain't hardly nothing but about ten acres of pin oaks and weeds. Right across the road from the river. Secluded as hell. You want to take a look at it?"

"Yes, that's what I had in mind. Today, hopefully."

The clerk rummaged in a drawer and found a pad of scratch paper. Very laboriously he sketched a crude map. I shoved it into a pocket and I thanked him. He said, "That old stone building's falling down. Used to be a monastery."

"Honest to God?"

The clerk grinned. "Yeah, that's the weirdest part of all. Carl Garvey owning an old monastery."

At the bottom of Geneva's Main Street hill I turned north on Route 25. Some three miles beyond St. Charles I reached a sign that said FOX RIVER ESTATES and there I swung left to follow a snaky, blacktopped route that eventually straightened out to make a run to the west. At a leaning concrete silo I made a right turn to the top of a long, gradual rise. Here I turned left to

99

plunge down a wicked roller-coaster type incline to the banks of the Fox.

The country grew desolate and I tooled along a narrow, dusty shoreline road for what may have been a quarter mile before an eight-foot stone wall loomed on my left. At this point I braked and rolled to where two huge, chipped, gray concrete pillars supported a pair of rusted gates. I pulled onto the shoulder and got out. The gates were chained and padlocked shut and the chain was enveloped in the undisturbed rust of years. A slender, weedy, graveled drive wound three hundred or more feet to the dim outlines of a large, crumbling stone building. It was a rambling structure and its windows had been boarded. There were no signs of life, not so much as a single bird, and the only sounds I heard were the occasional splashings of the Fox's diseased catfish. The suffocating heat of the day, the silence and the rotting-watermelon odor of the filthy, sluggish, algae-choked waters became downright oppressive. The area was drenched in contamination and decay and if this was nature somebody was perfectly welcome to my share of it.

I leaned against a concrete pillar to watch an automobile descend the steep hill to my right. The afternoon sun glinted blinding-bright on its windshield. It approached slowly at first but, at a distance of fifty or so yards, it accelerated sharply to roar past in a churning cloud of dust and gravel. It was a black or dark-blue vehicle, probably a mid-size General Motors car, but the dust obscured both the driver and the rear license plate.

I watched it out of sight and then, in the heavy quiet of that river afternoon, I climbed into my car to begin the forty-five-minute return trip to Chicago. I was disappointed and strangely disturbed. Carl Garvey's monastery left a lot to be desired. Well, after all, what had I expected? Cowled men, Gregorian chants, the celestial thunderings of a mighty organ? Probably. Anticipation always exceeds realization and, what the hell, an abandoned monastery is an abandoned monastery.

I drove homeward, my spirits lifting with my return to the city. Things were looking up. That sudden influx of money had helped considerably and I'd have five hundred coming from Elizabeth Fudge when we pulled off the robbery of the century

MONASTERY NIGHTMARE

at Leffingwell Historical Museum. Best of all, *Monastery Nightmare* was sailing along in grand style and my brief look at Garvey's broken-down building had brought the certain knowledge that I had the book whipped. If it could slip past a couple of editors and if Buck's operation worked just half as well as he seemed to think it would I might be standing on the rim of a minor league bonanza.

I parked the Caprice in front of my building and went in. Smoke filled the vestibule and staircase. I went up the steps on the double and rushed into my apartment. I found a naked Crystal Ball in the kitchen, bending over an open oven. She looked up and said, "Luke, this damned stove is all screwed up! It *burns* things!"

I said, "For Christ's sake get a window open before we die of smoke inhalation!"

Crystal said, "We can't do that!"

I said, "Why the hell can't we?"

"Because, if we open a window, the neighbors will think there's something wrong."

"Screw the neighbors! Crystal, what's in that oven?"

"Just a licorice pie."

"Who ever heard of a licorice pie?"

"Well, Luke, there's a first time for everything."

"Crystal, why don't you just stick with Shakespeare and stay out of the kitchen?" I raised a window and stuck my head out. When I'd stopped coughing I said, "Heaven sends good meat but the Devil sends cooks."

"Did Shakespeare say that?"

"No, it was Garrick."

"The ball player?"

"What ball player?"

"Lou Garrick."

"It was William Garrick."

"Who's William Garrick?"

"I'm not sure but he certainly knows what he's talking about."

Crystal took my hand. She said, "Luke, I have a scrumptious idea."

"What's that? Licorice *soup*?"

101

Ross H. Spencer

"Huh-uh. Let's go to bed."

I said, "Okay."

Hell, if you can't beat 'em, *join* 'em. I wondered if that was from Shakespeare.

33

*P*amela Frost was wearing a charcoal dress with a broad scarlet sash at the waist. The charcoal dress was just dandy but she could have made it through the evening without that sash. Encircling her more than ample middle it looked like a scarlet equator. We were in the dining room of the Brass Bull on North Canal Street, one of Chicago's better downtown restaurants. The place was beautifully appointed, the atmosphere cordial, the lights low, the conversation subdued and a blue-gowned, white-haired lady wearing a pince-nez sat at an organ, drifting through a lengthy medley of Viennese waltzes. Pamela Frost was drinking old-fashioneds minus the fruit and I was working on a string of vodka martinis. I said, "With your handicap how can you possibly operate a literary agency?"

"I've been totally blind for less than a year but my eyes had been failing for quite some time. My adjustment to darkness was a gradual thing and by no means as difficult as it would have been had I been suddenly stricken."

"Glaucoma?"

"No, glaucoma's treatable. Hereditary retinal degeneration isn't. You just wait for the lights to go out."

"What about transportation, correspondence, manuscripts? How do you handle those?"

"I have a steady cabdriver who takes me both ways and sees me in and out. There's a typing service across the hall from my office and the girls have been just wonderful. A lady in my apartment building reads manuscripts to me. I get along." I shook my head in admiration. This was a determined, highly

103

intelligent woman who would get things done and to hell with the obstacles. She'd missed her calling in life. She should have been a man. She changed the subject. "You really ought to bear down on your writing, Luke. You're extremely talented. You have a genuine feeling for words and you don't waste them in order to pad a manuscript. That's the trouble with today's writing market. The reader wants bulk for his money and our authors comply by saying in ten pages what could have been said in a single paragraph."

"Garvey didn't."

"No, if Carl had written *Gone With the Wind* he'd have come out with two hundred pages. He'd have gotten even less from *For Whom the Bell Tolls*. Words for the sake of being wordy never impressed Carl. Did you ever start a Garvey book and put it down?"

"Once. Miss Hadley caught me reading *Death by Ecstasy* in English Class. I finished it during a detention period."

"You need someone to assist you with structure and pace, someone who'll scratch your back and sock the spurs to you every so often."

"You're saying that two heads are better than one."

"Why, certainly! So often two are *required*. All of us don't have that God-given writing-spark but some of us are excellent mechanics. We can't fly the airplane but we can *fix* it. I've never had a word published but I can assist others."

"You're a mechanic?"

"Luke, I'm one of the best in the business." She wasn't thumping her chest, she'd said it matter-of-factly and I believed her.

I said, "Pam, if I had the money I'd be on the first Suva-bound freighter out of Frisco."

"Suva? Suva, *Fiji*? *Why*?"

"To write. To find peace and write. I've been to Fiji and I loved it."

"Why a freighter?"

"It's the only way to travel. The price is right, the food is great and you're not up to your knees in tourists."

"I've heard that."

104

MONASTERY NIGHTMARE

"I did some time as a merchant seaman and I've never made a trip but what we carried three or four passengers."

Pamela Frost smiled her toothy, hungry smile. She said, "Maybe I'll come along. I'll be folding my agency shortly."

"No good without Garvey?"

"That's true but there's more to it than that. I'm fifty, I'm weary of the grind, I've invested wisely and I have an inheritance due. Aren't the Fijis heavily commercialized now?"

"I suppose so. I haven't been there in a long time, but I'd imagine that Suva Point is pretty much the same. That's where I'd want to live. Suva Point. Beautiful place."

Pamela Frost's appetite was 20–20. I watched her go through a thirty-five-dollar lobster tail the way a cougar goes through a lamb chop. We ordered double Gallianos on the rocks and we nipped at them between sips of black coffee. She said, "Some evening you must visit me. We'll talk about Suva Point. I've never seen the Southern Cross."

I said, "I'll be glad to." I was completely serious. She was an interesting woman and she could help me. I had a lot to learn about writing.

She said, "What will you be drinking?"

"Whatever you'll be pushing."

Pamela Frost smiled and reached for her thick white cane. She said, "Luke, you won't be able to drink what I'll be pushing."

34

Crystal Ball met me at the door. Stark naked. Except for her bayonet-heeled pumps. Her breasts protruded hard-nippled and her dark-amber eyes were bright with anticipation. She said, "Did you bring licorice?"

I said, "They were all out."

"Who was all out?"

"Everybody. I think the licorice factory's on strike."

Crystal said, "Damn those unions!"

I said, "Anyway, licorice is an aphrodisiac."

"I didn't know that."

"If there's one thing you don't need it's an aphrodisiac."

Crystal sighed a martyr's sigh. She took me by the hand and pulled me toward the bedroom. She said, "Oh, well, we'll just have to do the best we can with what we've got." There was a bit of the philosopher about Crystal. The influence of Shakespeare, I had no doubt.

Later, in the darkness, I lay listening to her rhythmic breathing, looking into the past. Many years ago our ship had put into Suva for repairs. By the time the parts had arrived and been installed nearly three weeks had elapsed and I'd fallen hopelessly in love with Suva Point. I'd seen the little white one-story dwellings along the shore of the Pacific, I'd chatted with their owners and drank gin and tonic on their screened porches. I'd watched the tides roll in, the sun sink and the moon come up. I'd experienced the awesome savagery of tropical storms, I'd listened to the natives sing "Isa Lei" deep into the liquid night and I'd realized that I was as close to Heaven as most men ever get.

MONASTERY NIGHTMARE

I'd missed Suva Point since the day we'd hoisted anchor. It owned an acre in the green pastures of my memory and I'd often wondered how it might be to live there with enough money to make ends meet, trying to write something of middling consequence and sitting on a beach knoll in the late evenings, keeping tabs on the Southern Cross. The dream of Suva Point had stayed with me but now I knew that if I was destined to return to the Fiji Islands it would have to be with Crystal. She snuggled close to me, very soft and smooth and warm. I squeezed her fanny and she threw an arm over my shoulder and a leg over my hip. She mumbled, "There's beggary in the love that can be reckoned." I could see her with Shakespeare on the beach at Suva Point.

Clothed, of course.

35

*B*arb pulled her Mercedes into the alley beside Bessie Barnum's Circus Tap, parking immediately ahead of Stash Dubinski's black Mercury. Stash would be in the Circus Tap, drinking Stroh's and keeping his fingers crossed. Across 72nd Court to the east loomed the imposing rear of the Leffingwell Historical Museum and we had a clear view of its parking lot. The humid night was destitute of stars and in its gloom mists writhed like gray reptiles. I sat next to Barb and watched tiny sweat beads begin to form on the hood of the car. From down the street the pink glow of a sodium-vapor streetlight filtered through lank leaves to create eerie shadow arrangements. The interior of the Mercedes had all the conviviality of a Russian mausoleum and you could have carved your initials in the silence. At last Geraldine Swisher spoke from the rear seat. "Research tells us that historical museums are the least robbed of all public-frequented institutions."

Nobody responded to this pearl of information. The tension was getting to us. I thought of London and Fu Manchu and Jack the Ripper and Dr. Moriarty. Then I thought of Elmwood Park and Elizabeth Fudge and Geraldine Swisher and Candy Stoneman and I wished to Christ I was in London. I could hear Elizabeth Fudge rustling around behind me. I glanced over my shoulder and recoiled against the dashboard. I said, "My God, take off that ridiculous ski mask! You'll scare somebody to death and we'll all go up for murder!"

Barb stabbed me in the ribs with her elbow. She said, "Don't be irritable."

MONASTERY NIGHTMARE

I said, "Well, goddammit, she has to cross 72nd Court and if anybody sees her they'll think the Martians have landed!"

Barb said, "Cool it, Luke! This is no time for dissension!"

Elizabeth Fudge said, "Young man, do you realize that I am crusading for the restoration of my dignity?"

Geraldine Swisher said, "Research establishes that such crusades are not uncommon. Witness our own nation's crusade against taxation without representation."

I said, "Witness, also, Lizzie Borden's crusade for the right to reduce people to confetti with an axe." A railroad whistle soared high and forlorn in the darkness. I heard a distant bell and somewhere a dog howled a brokenhearted howl. At last headlights flashed on in the Leffingwell parking lot and I looked at my watch: 11:56. I motioned to Elizabeth Fudge. "Get it in gear, Bonnie! That'll be Rudy Garson checking out."

Elizabeth Fudge got out of the car and knelt beside it.

I said, "What the hell's she doing, checking the tires?"

Candy Stoneman said, "She's praying for divine assistance."

I said, "Well, Jesus Christ, she's lost her religion, she's about to commit a goddam robbery and she's praying for divine assistance!" Barb nailed me again with her elbow. I said, "Look, if she doesn't get moving *all* of us better start praying for divine assistance!"

Elizabeth Fudge rose and slipped gauntly into the mists. I watched her depart and felt an ominous chill skitter up my spine. This was one dangerous female. All females are dangerous but Elizabeth Fudge had something extra on the ball. She was the aggressive type, the kind that always manages to get it done wrong.

I checked my watch. Midnight sharp. Fudge would be in the museum now. If she didn't fall down the stairs and break her goddam neck we should be on our way in three or four minutes. An automobile turned into the Leffingwell parking lot. A uniformed man got out. Sweet suffering Jesus! For the first time in a year of Sundays Clint Kelly had come to work on *time*!

Candy Stoneman said, "This simply can't be as bad as it seems."

I said, "Why, of course not. It's infinitely worse."

Geraldine Swisher said, "There's hope. Research informs us

109

that it is completely possible for two people to occupy a large building and never meet."

I said, "Well, that may be true in some cases but I will bet you thirty-two dollars that this ain't one of them."

We sat. Then we sat some more. Geraldine Swisher didn't say anything. I was very glad of this.

Then things happened. A light winked on in the south wing of Leffingwell Historical Museum. There was a shout. There was a shriek of pain. There was a grinding, stuttering sound followed by a great clattering roar. The rear doors of the museum were blasted from their hinges. Down the steps of the staid institution bounded a 1932 Packard automobile, Elizabeth Fudge crouched low over the steering wheel, her gray hair streaming behind her, her ski mask dangling from one ear, her spectacles gleaming. The old vehicle lurched southward, careening into the pink glow of the streetlight, backfiring and belching great jagged sheets of flame and clouds of oily black smoke. It was a scene that would have sent Dante directly to Alcoholics Anonymous.

Clint Kelly stumbled into the shattered doorway of the building. He had a pistol in one hand and an arrow in one buttock. He emptied his gun in the general direction of everything. The sodium-vapor streetlight went out in a shower of slivered glass. So did Stash Dubinski's windshield.

Geraldine Swisher said, "Research indicates that it is unlikely that Elizabeth will catch more than three successive green traffic signals."

I said, "Well, I am indeed very sorry to hear this because that vehicle has no brakes and its hand-throttle is rusted open."

Sirens wailed in the distance and I nudged Barb. I said, "Let's get the hell out of here."

Barb started the engine and looked at me quizzically. "Where?"

I said, "Don't get into trivialities."

Geraldine Swisher said, "There's one thing that's terribly wrong with this situation."

I said, "Strange. I could have sworn that I've counted seventy-five."

Barb whipped the Mercedes out of the alley and into Eliza-

110

MONASTERY NIGHTMARE

beth Fudge's smoking wake. She said, "Geraldine, let's not discuss research at this time."

Geraldine said, "Good Lord, Barbara, who's discussing research? Elizabeth doesn't know how to *drive!*"

36

Abe Langberg's Elmwood Park Fresh Fish Market on North Avenue had closed at six o'clock but Elizabeth Fudge had reopened it shortly after midnight. The tail end of Rabies Razzano's 1932 Packard projected from what remained of a display window. The night sizzled with flashing red and blue lights and the Elmwood Park fire engines were beginning to arrive. Barb screeched her Mercedes to a halt three-quarters of a block beyond the scene of the catastrophe and the four of us piled out to move rapidly toward Langberg's. Geraldine Swisher said, "Research serves to place the 1932 Packard very high on the all-time list of safely constructed passenger vehicles. Only a few 1932 Packard drivers have died as the result of collisions."

I said, "Don't be too optimistic. Abe Langberg ain't here yet."

A windshieldless black Mercury fishtailed, bounced over the curb and stopped just short of the sidewalk. A big man jumped out to race through the gathering crowd, straight-arming people like an NFL running back. He plunged into the rubble of Abe Langberg's Elmwood Park Fresh Fish Market. In a few moments he plunged right back out. His pants were ripped, his hair was full of mortar dust and there was a limp mackerel stuck in his shirt collar. He saw me and rushed to me, grabbing me by the shoulders. His eyes were wide and wild. He said, "Luke! What the hell happened, Luke?"

I shrugged. I said, "Well, maybe we better begin with Clint Kelly showing up for work on time."

MONASTERY NIGHTMARE

Stash Dubinski said, "Yeah, she shot him in the ass with one of William Tell's arrows. They can't get the damn thing out!"

"Yeah, arrows are a bitch to get out."

"Not the arrow! It's that goddam apple core!" Stash gnashed his teeth. He said, "How the hell did I ever get into this mess?"

Candy Stoneman said, "The automobile can be repaired. Certainly Rabies Razzano carried insurance."

Stash said, "Jesus Christ, lady, Razzano got killed in a shoot-out with the FBI in 1934!"

Geraldine Swisher said, "Yes, but he must have had a grace period."

I said, "To hell with the car! We'd better drag that whippy old broad out of there!"

Stash shook his head vehemently. He said, "Langberg's back door is wide open! She's long gone and so are the Red Sea Documents!"

37

We sat on the living room couch surveying the ruins of one of Mama Mia's large cheese, sausage and mushroom pizzas. Crystal hadn't been talking much and I said, "Why all the silence?"

She munched absentmindedly on a pizza crust and in a while she said, "Silence is the perfectest herald of joy: I were but little happy if I could say how much."

I said, "So much for Shakespeare. Any other reasons?"

"Uh-huh. I've been wondering if there was ever a licorice pizza."

"No survivors if there was." I looked her over. I said, "Tell me, does pizza taste better when you're naked?"

"It's just great until you drop a hot mushroom into your lap. Where did you find that old Bible?"

"Under the bed. It was my mother's. It says, 'Thou shalt not screw out of wedlock.'"

"Things without remedy should be without regard: what's done is done."

"You know, I had a hunch on that."

"If you're going to turn Catholic that's the wrong Bible. It's a King James version."

"I'm trying to figure a way to encode the Professor James nuclear formula in my story. I thought I might use the Bible as a crypto base."

"Shakespeare helped with the translation of the King James version."

"I doubt that very much."

114

MONASTERY NIGHTMARE

"Honest to God, Luke! He even left proof."

"Phooey."

"All right, smart aleck, find the Book of Psalms!"

"No problem. Now what?"

"Look for the forty-sixth psalm. Got it?"

"Got it."

"Okay, in the forty-sixth psalm what's the forty-sixth word from the beginning?"

I ran my forefinger across the column. I said, "Shake."

"Correct. Now, what's the forty-sixth word from the end?"

I checked it out and said, "In."

"No, no, no! You're counting that *sēläh* at the finish."

"Of course I'm counting that *sēläh* at the finish. It's a word, isn't it?"

"Yes, but, you see, Luke, it has no bearing on the text. It's ancient Chaldean translating to 'be secure' or 'think on this' or some damn thing. You can't count *sēläh*."

"The hell I can't count *sēläh*. It's there and I'm gonna count it."

"Well, just throw it out and count backwards to the forty-sixth word."

"Crystal, I don't *want* to throw it out."

"All right, damn you, what's the forty-*seventh* word?"

"Spear."

"So there you are, wise guy! Shake-spear! See?"

I said, "Well, my God, that's ridiculous! You use a goofy system like that and my grandmother could prove that she wrote 'The Star Spangled Banner.' Only she didn't. It was Francis Scott Key."

"Just the words, Luke. John Stafford Smith wrote the music."

"Okay, Crystal."

"Originally it was called 'The Anacreontic Song.' "

"Oh, goody."

"Anacreon was a Greek poet and there was this London club named after him and the boys would meet there and get drunk and sing John Stafford Smith's song."

"Wonderful. Just flat-out wonderful."

"Sometimes they used naughty words."

"Why those dirty bastards!"

115

"I know a chorus or two."

"Crystal?"

"Yes, Luke?"

"Shut up, for Christ's sake!"

Crystal giggled. She put her peroxide-blonde head on my shoulder. She said, "Oh, this is what I like about us!"

"What's that?"

"It will not fit my tongue, this understanding which I do not understand."

"Crystal, how did you ever get so wound up over Shakespeare?"

"That wasn't Shakespeare. That was *me*. It just came to mind. Since I met you it happens all the time."

I closed the Bible and placed it on the coffee table. Our conversation had been meaningless but it had given me an idea.

And I was in love with Crystal Ball. I said, "Let's go to bed."

Crystal's voice broke. She said, "Luke, that's the first time you've ever asked me."

38

*I*n the next few days I took on a couple of divorce cases and blew both of them. I got knocked half-silly in Fargo's Saloon on the south side when I was struck in the temple by a cue-ball. My car was sideswiped in a supermarket parking lot and I lost five pounds eating licorice omelettes and doing my damndest to satisfy the multitudinous sexual whims of Crystal Ball. But I finished *Monastery Nightmare*.

I'd woven Carl Garvey's bleak old riverside shambles into the story, describing it as best I could from my memories of that steamy afternoon north of St. Charles, Illinois. Beyond that, I'd taken great pains in the coding of the nuclear formula of Professor James:

1-3-7/1-8-2/1-11-4/1-1-5/‡‡‡ 1-15-4/1-4-1/1-9-2/3-9-4‡‡‡
1-14-2/1-3-3/1-11-4/1-3-7/1-8-1/1-1-4/1-3-6‡‡‡ 1-15-4/2-1-2‡‡‡
1-9-1/3-7-3/3-9-4/1-3-2‡‡‡ 1-9-1/1-1-2/1-1-5/1-1-5/1-11-4/
1-3-7/1-1-4/1-11-3‡‡‡ 3-6-2/1-4-1/1-3-3/‡‡‡ 1-14-2/1-11-4/
1-9-1/1-9-1/1-11-4/1-1-2/1-1-3‡‡‡ 1-14-2/1-1-4/1-1-5/1-3-7/
1-1-4/1-3-3/1-3-4/1-11-4/1-9-1/1-9-1/1-1-4‡‡‡ 1-1-2/1-3-6/
1-5-3‡‡‡ 1-1-2/1-1-5/1-1-5/1-4-1/1-11-1/1-11-4/1-1-2/1-3-7/
1-1-4/1-1-5‡‡‡

I'd reveled in the entire effort. Crystal had stayed right with me, start to finish, gently nagging me when I lagged, phoning me at the office when she struck snags, typing and retyping and never beefing about changes or corrections. Then, suddenly, it had been behind us and I'd damned near wept when we'd put it into its box. I'd felt no counterfeiter's guilt. To me, probably the world's number-one Hillary Condor enthusiast, it seemed appropriate that I be the author of the great man's final adventure. I'd tied up a big bunch of loose ends. I'd returned the few surviving villains from previous volumes and I'd wiped the bastards out—the Wasp Woman who stung United States senators to death with a stinger concealed precisely where you'd expect a stinger to be concealed, the Chameleon whose ability to change the color of his skin at will enabled him to stir up racial strife the world over, Dr. Boris Scraggovitch and his boomba-boomba plants—these and others walked my plank along with Brother Sigfried and Brother Luigi, the two mad bogus monks implacably dedicated to the enslavement of mankind.

I'd done better than that. I'd summoned the parson for Hillary Condor and his devoted, three months pregnant Miriam Mission. The wedding ceremony had been conducted in the Oval Office of the White House with the President serving as Condor's best man while, on the lawn, the United States Senate had warbled "I Love You Truly" to the accompaniment of the Philadelphia Philharmonic Orchestra under the dewy-eyed direction of Jane Fonda. Then I'd retired the loving couple to the rustic sanctuary of Condor's Nest and I'd set Hillary to work on his memoirs.

I'd done a lot of things that Carl Garvey probably wouldn't have approved of but, what the hell, I was writing this book, not Carl Garvey, and, this way, dyed-in-the-wool Hillary Condor followers wouldn't lose any sleep wondering about what had happened to whom. This was the grand finale. There wouldn't *be* any more Hillary Condor stories and I'd walked away from the undertaking feeling that I'd given Garvey's paper people more happiness than their creator would have ever seen fit to spare.

Then I'd met Buck Westerville at the Pelican Club. He'd leafed rapidly through the manuscript, shrugged and said, "Luke, I'm no judge. I'm trusting in your know-how."

I'd said, "It should pass."

It did. Within a week Buck stopped at the office to hand me a bulging white envelope. He said, "Cash. Count it. Five percent

MONASTERY NIGHTMARE

of a twenty-grand advance payment. Now we wait for the kettle to boil. We just wait."

I'd always been good at waiting but for just a moment I could hear the lulling rustle of the night tides on the beach at Suva Point.

39

*T*he early August afternoon was warm and overcast. I was at the Sherwood Forest Pub talking to Mary O'Rourke when she groaned under her breath and signaled with her eyes toward the entrance. Kenny Blossom was swaggering in. He whacked me on the shoulder and said, "Hiya, Luke, what's new?" One of these days he'd do that and I'd just have to get up and knock him flat on his fat ass. Kenny's narrow-brimmed white Stetson was pushed well to the back of his kinky blond head and his watery-blue eyes shone with good spirits. His sleeves were rolled to the elbows and above a brass-studded wristband his fat woman was still giving his Brahma bull more than the poor bastard could handle. His denim jacket was open and his pearl-handled six-shooter glittered threateningly. I wondered if he'd ever fired the damned thing. I motioned to Mary for a round of Stroh's and a smile twitched Kenny's meatloaf face. He said, "Hey, you hear about the old broad who swiped the car out of Leffingwell Museum?"

I said, "Must have missed it."

Mary brought the beer and said, "That's old news, Luke. Some woman got into the museum and a guard caught her and she shot him. It was in the papers."

"Did she kill him?"

Kenny guffawed. "Naw, but he was sitting on a pillow for a while. She hit him in the fanny with an arrow and then she hopped into an antique car and drove right through the museum doors."

"They catch her?"

Monastery Nightmare

"They found what was left of the car. It ended up in a fish market out on North Avenue. By the time the cops got there the woman had took off with them documents."

Mary said, "What documents?"

"The Red Sea Documents. They're worth a pile of money." Kenny winked at me. He said, "I got it figured as an inside job."

Mary said, "I didn't read about any documents, just about the automobile she stole. It was an old Packard that belonged to some trigger-happy gangster."

Kenny took a big swallow of his beer. He said, "Well, I didn't really read it myself. My barber was telling me about it."

I said, "Maybe you should have gotten a haircut while he was talking."

Kenny said, "How's your love life, Luke?"

I said, "I'm too old for that kind of carrying on."

Kenny finished his beer and slipped from his barstool. He wiped his mouth and said, "Well, see you around, Luke."

When he was gone I said, "A rapid and welcome exit."

Mary said, "Not rapid enough. God, how I detest that bastard. He talks too much."

"He sure does." I'd gone through the papers with a fine-tooth comb and I'd seen no mention of the Red Sea Documents.

Mary said, "Oh, Luke, it nearly slipped my mind! I talked to Bertha Zane and she dropped in earlier today."

I said, "Bertha Zane?"

"The girl who works at Chicago Second National. She got what you wanted." Mary opened her purse and handed me a folded manila envelope. "This stuff's for June. She'll get the July report pretty soon."

I emptied the envelope onto the bar. The contents had to do with the Johnny Huskin Evangelistic Association checking account. There was a Xerox copy of the account statement and one-sided prints of thirty or so checks. I thumbed through them. Most had been written to benevolent organizations, the Salvation Army, the Little Brothers of the Poor, Alabama Flood Relief, Orphans of the Storm and so on but there was one that stopped me stone cold. It seemed to *glow*. It was made out in the amount of four hundred thousand dollars to the Children's Charities of Northern Borneo.

ROSS H. SPENCER

I glanced at the June statement. As of June 30 the Johnny Huskin Evangelistic Association account balance had stood at $38,086.73. One helluva far cry from a million.

Well, so much for my ability to judge human character. I wouldn't know an honest man from a busted bale of alfalfa. I jammed the stuff back into the envelope and pushed it across the bar to Mary. She said, "Was it what you expected?"

"Not at all and I'm glad."

Mary said, "Anytime I can help, Luke."

When I got back to my office the phone was ringing. It was Barb. I said, "What happened to that crackpot Elizabeth Fudge? Stash has to get those documents back! The display case is nearly ready and they're to be shown next month!"

"She's in Wisconsin, I believe. She goes up there to meditate. Luke, I'd might as well tell you—I'm calling from the house."

"Barb, you know better than that!"

"It doesn't matter now. If this telephone is bugged the jig is up. I just had a call from a man who knows about you and me."

"Say what?"

"It's the truth. He has it all, Luke—my name and address, your name and address and the fact that I've visited your apartment. What else does he need?"

"Money. How much?"

"He didn't get around to it. He wants to meet me. There are other considerations. He says that since I'm passing it out he wants to be dealt in."

"I'm a sonofabitch!"

"Oh, he isn't bashful. He gave me graphic descriptions of what he has in mind. Luke, this is a very sick man and I'm scared to death!"

"When does he want to meet you?"

"He said he'll be in touch."

"Okay, you meet him."

"Will you be there?"

"Of course. Maybe I can show him the error of his ways."

"Which means that you'll knock his brains out."

"It won't come to that. There's nothing yellower than a blackmailer. He'll fold up like a busted balloon."

Barb's voice quavered. "God, how bad can things get?"

122

MONASTERY NIGHTMARE

I said, "Don't sweat it. He's a rank amateur. Professionals don't operate like this. You'd never lay eyes on a pro. You'd have to make a drop."

"But how does he *know*?"

"There's a leak in your dyke. Candy Stoneman, maybe."

"Not a chance! She'd just be cutting off her nose to spite her face. I have more on Candy than Candy has on me. Besides, Candy doesn't need money. Her husband owns four automobile dealerships."

"Barb, we'll have to cool it a few degrees."

"I know that and I don't like it! Christ, I'll go nuts!"

"Tell me something. When Elizabeth Fudge took off with Rabies Razzano's Packard was there mention of the Red Sea Documents in the newspapers?"

"None! I checked those accounts very carefully."

"Okay, but I'm acquainted with a scuzzy private detective named Kenny Blossom who knows that the documents went with the car."

"Kenny who?"

"Kenny Blossom. He has an office on South State Street. I talked to him less than an hour ago."

"Nobody knew the documents were in that old car. Nobody but you and your friend from the museum."

"Nobody knew until Fudge wrecked the car. Then Fudge knew and Stash Dubinski blurted it out when he got to Langberg's Fish Market. After that, you were hep and so was Candy and so was Geraldine Swisher."

"Well, yes, but so was anyone else who was within earshot. Luke, I can't think straight. I feel like I'm caught up on a crazy, out-of-control carousel!"

"Settle down. Nobody's been murdered."

"Not yet, but if Johnny gets wind of this he'll go off the deep end. I know Johnny Huskin!"

"What's Candy's emergency number on her swinging nights?"

"I don't believe I should tell you that."

"Barb, *I'm* not being blackmailed, *you* are!"

"All right, just a moment." She gave me the number: 455-5340. She said, "Then you have to ask for Mr. Smith's room."

123

ROSS H. SPENCER

I said, "He'll be right in between Mr. Jones and Mr. Davis."

There was a weak smile in Barb's voice. "Yes, across from Mr. Brown."

I said, "Okay, get some rest." I hung up and found Mickey South's number in my address book. He was out but the girl said he'd call back in ten minutes. He called in five. I said, "I'm looking for an address to go with 455-5340."

"I'll get to you in twenty minutes, Luke." He got to me in ten. "You could have dialed it yourself. Jack Rabbit Motel on Mannheim Road in Franklin Park."

"There'll be an envelope at the Sherwood tomorrow."

"Thanks, Luke."

Mickey South was a very efficient young fellow. Much too efficient to be less than halfway up the Illinois Bell Telephone Company managerial ladder.

124

40

Monastery Nightmare hit the market in late August. At first I couldn't imagine the publishing industry moving that rapidly but then I remembered the Entebbe hostage rescue by Israeli special forces and how, within a couple of weeks, not one but *two* detailed Entebbe volumes were on the stands. Then, too, Buck Westerville had told me that the machinery was "greased all the way to Manhattan" and if the publisher, Wellington Books of New York City, had anticipated the book's arrival, its quick appearance seemed logical enough. It was a trim little volume of one hundred eighty-eight pages. Its dust jacket was a stark thing, black-and-white, a reproduction of the artist's excellent charcoal drawing, an old stone building, turreted, a gaunt, leafless tree silhouetted against a full moon that wallowed in a sea of menacing black clouds, two cowled figures on a distant hilltop. It was spooky as hell and I liked it. But it bore Carl Garvey's name, not mine, and I wondered if I'd ever know the thrill of seeing my own name on the cover of a hardbound book. I grinned wryly. Second-rate gumshoe Luke Lassiter, the would-be writer who'd turned out a professional-class hair-raiser in nothing flat, the man who wouldn't get a single line of credit for his accomplishment. Well, the hell with it. I'd take my kudos in United States currency. Westerville had assured me that there'd be no shortage of that.

I thought of the dedication I'd done for *Monastery Nightmare*.

ROSS H. SPENCER

To he who reads and thinks he sees
The all of which I tell
But reads again and then agrees
He read it not too well.

That, of course, had to do with the Professor James nuclear formula code. Buck Westerville wasn't the most honorable of men and the nuclear formula was an insurance policy I'd taken out, just in case. It was a simple enough bit of cryptography, childlike, really, but, without the key, even a Pentagon crew wouldn't get around the corner.

Lord, wouldn't it be something if there was enough money in all this hocus-pocus to send Crystal and me to Suva Point, away from the rat race and the pollution and the noise, where Crystal could founder herself on the writings of the Bard of Avon and I could nourish my shrinking soul with the sounds of surf, where I could drink myself giddy on the wines of star-splashed tropical nights, where I could write. Or try to. No more of this Hillary Condor foolishness. Observations, reflections, thoughts. Just pull the plug and let it all gush out. Somehow I felt that locked within me was something to say. Perhaps it would be poetry. Not avant-garde trash. Mine would rhyme and make sense, it would be on the order of the works of Kipling, Riley, Noyes, Whittier and Service, writing that brought the reader a thought and a smile or a tear.

Well, enough of the pipe dreams. I stuffed *Monastery Nightmare* into my jacket pocket and took the stairs down to Adams Street. My elevator still wasn't working.

41

*T*aking a woman to bed is no great trick. Living with her is another ball game. The average female has been brought up to believe that she is an intricate and temperamental creature. She's taught that she has prerogatives transcending all rules, divine rights, if you will, because she is a woman. Properly indoctrinated along these lines, the average woman does her very damndest to be intricate and temperamental whether she is intricate and temperamental or not, wielding her prerogatives as a crazed barbarian wields a bloody axe. Not so with Crystal Ball. If she was intricate and temperamental she kept it a secret and if she had prerogatives she didn't exercise them. More than lovers, we'd become friends. I felt that I'd known her since birth. We meshed. There were times when she exasperated me but dealing with licorice and Shakespeare was by no means as difficult as finding yourself staring at a tearful female who doesn't have the slightest idea what she's crying about.

It wasn't what Crystal *was* that mattered so much to me. It was what she *wasn't*. She didn't sulk, she wasn't given to mystic moods, she didn't whimper, she didn't weep and seek sympathy. She just came down the middle of the road, bright-eyed and bushy-tailed, helping when she could and getting the hell out of the way when she couldn't. A man can't ask for more than that.

One evening we walked over to Abe Glassman's place for a corned beef sandwich and a stein of beer and, for the first time since its appearance, Crystal mentioned *Monastery Nightmare*. She said, "How's it doing?"

ROSS H. SPENCER

I said, "I probably won't know until spring."

"Why so long?"

"That's the way publishing houses operate. The first royalty period will end in December and they won't report until March or April."

Crystal said, "Gosh, Luke, with all the books you've written, I'd think you could have given up being a detective long ago."

"*All* the books?"

"Sure. You have a bookcase full. But that isn't your picture. Whose is it?"

No point in going into it. I said, "Just a guy I used to know."

"You're a funny one, Luke. If I could write a book I'd be proud. I'd send them my real picture and I'd give them straight information. You just don't want publicity, I guess."

I shrugged and let it pass.

Crystal chewed contentedly on her corned beef sandwich for a minute. Then she said, "How did you ever settle on 'Carl Garvey' for a whatchacallit?"

"Pseudonym?"

"Uh-huh."

"I got it out of a telephone book."

"You could have done better than that. It's such a *plain* name." She sat, frowning. I could feel it coming. She said, "What's in a name? That which we call a rose by any other name would smell as sweet."

I nodded and finished my kosher pickle. Suddenly Crystal leaned across the table, her dark-amber eyes flaring. She said, "Who the hell typed all those other books?"

I said, "One of my landladies."

"Did she keep her clothes on?"

"She was seventy-six years old."

Crystal smiled into her beer stein. She said, "That's nice."

When we left Abe Glassman's I put my arm around her. I kept it there all the way home.

42

Barb called me at the office next morning. She said, "Everything okay?"

I said, "Okay here. Anything from the blackmailer?"

"Not a peep, but he's out there somewhere, I can *feel* him. I heard from Elizabeth Fudge a few minutes ago. She's at home."

"All right, what about the Red Sea Documents?"

"That's why I called. Luke, Elizabeth has read those papers over and over and she tells me that she's undergone a compelling and all-encompassing theological mesmerization."

"Tell her to call the paramedics. Stash has to get those documents back. He's about ready to blow his top!"

"You don't seem to understand, Luke. Elizabeth's been born again!"

"I thought she'd already been born again."

"Yes, this makes twice but she says that her second experience was far more powerful than the first. She realizes that she's been vindictive and that she must make amends. She's going to square up with the museum and Clint Kelly and Abe Langberg."

"How's she going to accomplish that?"

"Anonymously. Postal money orders. She tells me that her eyes have been opened and that she now believes in the Millennium and speaking in tongues."

"Barb, let's talk about the Red Sea Documents."

"Elizabeth intends to return the documents and William Tell's equipment herself."

"She's crazy! They'll arrest her scrawny old ass on the spot!"

129

ROSS H. SPENCER

"No, Luke, she wants to do it at night. You're going to have to get Elizabeth into Leffingwell Museum one more time."

I took a deep breath and said, "Now, Barb, you listen to me—"

She cut me off. "Luke, you *have* to do it! Otherwise Elizabeth is going to the Elmwood Park police with the entire story!"

"An ultimatum?"

"Exactly. It's Elizabeth's way or else."

"Jesus Christ, why didn't she leave those goddam documents in Razzano's car in the first place?"

"She wasn't aware that she had them. The impact of the collision drove them under her girdle."

"It should have rammed them up her ass!"

"It did. I was trying to put it delicately."

I cussed for two minutes and didn't use the same word twice. Barb remained silent. At last I said, "How much time do I get?"

"Not much. She's hot to trot."

I thought it over. I was like the guy who had the tiger by the tail. If he held on he was through and if he let go he was througher. I thought of the Lassiter family tradition and shrugged. I said, "All right, I'll take a shot at it."

130

43

That afternoon Itchy Balzino lumbered into the office with a smile and a big package. He grabbed my hand and crunched down on it until I saw stars. He dumped his package onto my desk and said, "Hey, kid, is turkey for Thanksgiving!"

I said, "Well, great, but Thanksgiving is damn near three months away."

"Is no problem. Just stick in freezer."

I stared at the gift dubiously. I said, "Ten-to-one Crystal stuffs it with licorice."

"You ought taste her licorice gravy."

"How is it?"

"Unusual." Itchy scratched his shoulder. He said, "So how's it go? You get along with Crystal real nice?"

"Real nice."

"Hey, is good for Crystal. Is also good for you. Is might be better for you than is good for Crystal." He sprawled on my sofa and plunked his enormous feet on the edge of my desk. Alligator shoes. Probably one alligator each. He said, "Hey, when you and Crystal get married, make babies? You not Catholic yet?"

"I'm nothing."

Itchy sat up and scratched his shin. "Nothings is kind making best Catholics. Fine Catholic boy marry Crystal prob'ly end up big house Oak Park, two baths, pool, new car, no doubt black Cadillac." He got to his feet and leaned over my desk. He said, "Hey, kid, think on it." His voice had a ring of sincerity.

I said, "Okay." So did mine.

ROSS H. SPENCER

Itchy went out and I put my ear to the turkey. It wasn't ticking.

My mind went back to a *Chicago Tribune* headline of a few years earlier. BALZINO RIVALS SLAIN IN NORTHSIDE PIZZA PARLOR.

Hail, Mary, full of grace.

44

*I*t was midnight at the table in the dimmest corner of Bessie Barnum's Circus Tap. It was midnight at the other tables too but that didn't mean a thing to Stash Dubinski and me. Our midnight was the blackest of all. We were barreled to the scuppers and Stash stared at me with the bloodshot eyes of a mortally wounded buffalo. He said, "Luke, this is loco! I wish I'd never heard of the fucking Red Sea!"

I said, "That makes three of us."

"You and me and who the hell else?"

"The Pharaoh."

"Screw the Pharaoh. What about you and me?"

"Stash, you got the ball."

"Yeah, fourth and fifty on my own one-yard line. I tried to call that witch this afternoon. She's probably out shooting people in the ass with her archery set. All I got was a bunch of organ music and some guy speaking Latin."

"What did he say?"

"How the hell should I know? Something like '*in nomine et patris filii et spiritus sancti.*'"

"That was Edgar."

"Is Edgar Catholic?"

"Just when he drinks. Stash, this is our only way out. Fudge is determined to put those Red Sea Documents back and if she can't return them in person she's going to turn herself in at the Elmwood Park Police Station."

Stash shuddered. He said, "Good God, Luke, if we give that raving lunatic another shot at Leffingwell there just ain't no

133

ROSS H. SPENCER

telling what could happen." He looked at me darkly. He said, "You just got to remember that we got a 155mm howitzer and a World War II bomber in there!"

I shrugged. "Well, suit yourself. Either Elizabeth Fudge gets into Leffingwell Museum in a hurry or the whole crew winds up in the Elmwood Park bastille."

Stash sat with his hands folded, rotating his thumbs. He sighed resignedly and said, "Okay, Luke, but she'll have to go in through the skylight. The superintendent had time-locks installed on all the doors and if we pop one of those it'll be a dead giveaway that I'm in on the deal."

"How can she use the skylight when we can't put her on the roof?"

"There's a way to get her up there. Like I told you, Lennie Neurotkowski got the Leffingwell roof and gutters contract."

"That doesn't put Elizabeth Fudge on the roof."

"Sure, it does! Late next week Lennie's boys are gonna tear off the old gutters and get set to hit the ball. Lennie got about a million ways to save money and one of 'em is gonna get your pet centipede back into Leffingwell."

"I'm listening."

Stash hauled out his ballpoint pen and drew a large square on a napkin. He made an X at an end of the square and circled it. He said, "At the southwest corner of the building Lennie will have this rope and pulley arrangement which will be attached to a boom on the roof. That'll be how he gets materials up to his workers."

"What about it?"

"It's different, that's what about it. Lennie uses water to hoist the stuff."

"I don't follow you."

"Well, the rope goes over the pulley and Lennie got an old bathtub hooked to one end of the rope."

"A *bath*tub?"

"Yeah, the kind like your grandmother used to have. You remember them monsters that had lion's feet for legs? They was a yard wide and about four feet tall."

"I don't think my grandmother ever took a bath. What's on the other end of the rope?"

134

MONASTERY NIGHTMARE

"Another old bathtub. They put the roofing materials in the bathtub that's on the ground and a guy on the roof grabs a hose and he puts water in the top tub. As soon as the water in the top tub outweighs the materials in the bottom tub the top tub goes down and the materials come up to the roof."

"Then what?"

"Then they tie the bottom tub to a tree and they drain it. When they want to send up more stuff they throw it into the lower tub, release the rope and put water in the upper tub. That's how it works, plain old see-saw principle. Them antique bathtubs can hold way the hell over two hundred gallons of water and Lennie can hoist damn near a ton of materials without nobody hardly even moving a muscle."

"I see. No ladders, no climbing, no manpower, nothing but an old bathtub full of water."

"You know it! The museum even pays for the *water*! Lennie Neurotkowski's a sharp customer! Well, when they get the rain gutters off I'll wait till they go home and I'll go up on the roof and put a little water in that top tub. How much does this old maniac weigh, would you say?"

I said, "Oh, maybe eighty-five pounds tops. There isn't an ounce of meat on her."

Stash jotted some figures on the napkin. He said, "So eleven, twelve gallons of water will do it real nice. All you got to do is put this Elizabeth Fudge in the bottom tub, cut the retaining rope and she gets a slow, soft ride to the roof."

"So far, so good. Go on."

"I'll leave the skylight unlocked. She'll open it, go down a little ladder and take the stairs to the ground floor of the south wing."

"Fine, but how does she get out with time locks on the doors?"

"Simple. While she's returning the documents you drain two or three gallons of water out of the lower tub and when she climbs into the top tub she comes down sweet and gentle."

I smiled and shook my head. "Stash, you're some kind of genius! What about Clint Kelly?"

Stash grinned a grizzly bear grin. He said, "Don't you worry about Clint Kelly. I know where Clint lives and I'm gonna steal the rotor out of his distributor."

135

45

The *Chicago Globe*'s literary critic, Matthew Ostergold, wrote that *Monastery Nightmare* was far and away the best of Carl Garvey's Hillary Condor series. He lamented the fact that it was "the final curtain call for the thrill-master who has dominated fiction's macho peninsula for more than two decades." Then Ostergold carried on something fierce through several tearful columns and this pleased me in spite of the fact that I had it on good authority that he was just a shade on the fruity side of the tree. Whatever Ostergold was, he spearheaded a critics' stampede and *Monastery Nightmare* was fifth in Chicagoland hardcover sales and ninth nationally. Foreign publishers were said to be snapping it up, the paperback industry was supposedly making sizable offers and four motion picture studios were locked in a bidding war for the property.

Monastery Nightmare wasn't that good and I knew it. It probably didn't rate with the authentic Hillary Condor stuff. The thing was that Carl Garvey was gone and now came the tributes he'd never received while living. Syndicated columnists took notice of the book, as did major news magazines. The Friday "Fiction Review" dedicated a half dozen pages to Garvey, and *Monastery Nightmare* was into a second printing with the ink barely dry on the first. Book reviewers the nation over had suddenly managed to discover new depths and hidden, mystic meanings in everything Garvey had written, interpreting it as veiled prophecy from a superintellect. The new Garvey popularity was generating important money and Buck Westerville's venture was beginning to look like a stroke of genuine

136

MONASTERY NIGHTMARE

genius but there were moments when I found myself wishing that it hadn't attained such brushfire proportions. I had a premonition that somewhere along the line somebody would become a bit too curious.

I am very good at premonitions.

46

*B*uck Westerville came into my office carrying a brown plastic folder and sweating profusely. He said, "Damn it, Luke, when are they going to fix that elevator?"

"When do I get my cut from *Monastery Nightmare?*"

"That'll take a while."

"So will the elevator. How does the book look?"

"Fantastic! Wellington's printed a half million. If only half of them sell you're good for over a hundred grand. We did it up brown, baby!"

"What about foreign rights, paperbacks and the movie people?"

"That's all in the mill. Sticky stuff. The movie rights could hit the moon."

"Who's negotiating it?"

Buck's smile was mysterious. "We'll do all right, don't worry about it."

"How's about a few grand on account?"

"Luke, when it happens it'll happen big and we'll be rolling in money but right now we just gotta hang on." He raised a hopeful forefinger and said, "However, I have something that will keep the wolf from your door."

"No more books, Buck. That'd be going to the well once too often."

"Right! This is a missing persons matter. It'll produce your hundred-and-a-half a day plus expenses and maybe you can stretch it all the way to payday."

138

MONASTERY NIGHTMARE

I said, "Who am I looking for?"

Buck put a match to his corncob pipe and grinned. He said, "Are you ready for this?"

"Shoot."

"Carl Garvey."

After a lengthy silence I swore. I said, "Knock it off, Buck! Garvey's dead."

"Sure, he's dead but my client thinks maybe he isn't."

"Who's your client?"

"Sorry, Luke, privileged information."

"Privileged information, my ass! You're talking to the guy who wrote *Monastery Nightmare!*"

Buck spread his hands, palms up. "Okay, okay, don't get hostile! Empire State Casualty Insurance out of New York."

"How the hell come?"

"Garvey was insured with Empire State for a hundred grand with a double indemnity accidental death clause."

"A heart attack doesn't come under the heading of accidental death."

"No, but drowning does."

"Empire State figures it's getting screwed? Fraud? Staged disappearance?"

"They regard it as a possibility. Garvey won't be legally dead until he's gone seven years. That gives Empire time to play with it and they like the odds. A few grand against two hundred thousand."

I said, "And it was *Monastery Nightmare* that kicked over the beehive."

Buck said, "Just think what this could do for sales."

I said, "I don't like it. Eventually Empire State will put a man in here and he could snaff the whole show."

"No sweat. Just go through the motions. Do the things you'd do if you were *really* looking for Carl Garvey. Be a little obvious. Scribble me a weekly report and make it interesting. We want it to look good."

"But, actually, I'm dogging it?"

"Oh, sure. Garvey's dead, any fool knows that."

"I'm getting a hundred-fifty a day. What are you charging Empire State?"

139

ROSS H. SPENCER

"Two-fifty." Buck tossed the brown plastic folder onto my desk. "Information from Empire State on Garvey. Got to be thorough, y'know. Happy trails, Luke!" He winked and went out, one of the great sharpshooters of his day.

47

Crystal perched naked on the arm of the sofa. She said, "Itchy thinks we should get married."

I said, "I know that. He also thinks I should turn Catholic."

"And *I* know *that*. Why don't you?"

"Because I'm not wearing a white suit to First Communion, that's why."

"Oh, don't be silly! That's only for children."

"Don't bet on it. I got a hunch that Itchy's a stickler for all the goodies."

Crystal put a hand on my shoulder. She said, "Luke, my mother's dead and I'm Itchy's only kid. I'm all he has and he'd be very good to us if we did it his way. He's dying to see me married and pregnant."

I sat with my elbows on my knees and my head in my hands, saying nothing.

After a long time Crystal said, "Luke?" Her voice was faint. I said, "Yeah?"

"Luke, all that's left is the getting married part."

I felt the blood drain from my face. I looked up and said, "Oh, my God!"

Crystal nodded. "That's exactly what *I* said." She stroked the back of my neck. She said, "Only I didn't turn pale."

48

*I*t was a gray, dismal September afternoon and I was at my desk, riffling through Buck Westerville's brown plastic folder. In it were Garvey's standard dust-jacket photograph, a brief résumé of his twenty-some-year writing career and a few odds and ends of trivia. The file had been assembled by Empire State Casualty and it wasn't worth much to an investigator working out of Chicago. Garvey's old address and phone number had been listed and they represented all I'd really be able to hang my hat on, whether I was seriously looking for Garvey or faking it. There was brief mention of his literary agent, Pamela Frost. There were comments from editors at Wellington Books, nothing of value, just personal impressions. These people had come to regard Carl Garvey as a rather mild individual, not at all the type to be writing the blood, thunder and sex stuff he'd churned out over the years. They'd noted that he'd been extremely affable so long as manuscript revisions weren't requested. Garvey detested revising and he became irate at the mere suggestion. According to the Wellington editors Garvey loathed the city of New York and he'd never once set foot in Wellington's offices. I saw samples of his handwriting, short notes to Wellington personnel, pleasant enough in tone, done in tight straight-up-and-down strokes. People who write in that fashion are independent, stand-on-their-own-two-feet types, or so I'd read in the books on handwriting analysis.

I closed the folder and pushed it away from me. I'd get the farce under way by contacting Garvey's widow. She lived in a condominium near Lincoln Park and I checked the folder for

MONASTERY NIGHTMARE

the telephone number. I dialed it and let it ring a dozen times before hanging up to watch my office door swing open.

A woman stood framed in the doorway. She was very beautiful with medium-length black hair, tawny gold complexion and thoughtful, wide-set blue eyes. Her nose was small, slightly uptilted, and her mouth was soft, red rose in hue and texture, the lower lip being slightly on the bee-stung order, the kind that's supposed to indicate sensuality and usually does. She was exquisitely assembled, full-bosomed, slim-waisted, long-legged, and she moved with the velvety grace of a young leopardess. She wore a crisp baby-blue blouse, a tailored white skirt and blue suede pumps. Halfway to my desk she hesitated. She said, "Mr. Luke Lassiter?" I nodded and stood, motioning her to the wooden chair. She thanked me and sat, crossing perfect legs and demurely tugging the hem of her skirt down over her knee. When she smiled my heart did a double backflip. She said, "Mr. Lassiter, do you look for missing people?"

"Yes, I look but, unfortunately, I don't always find them. No guarantees."

She put out her hand and I took it. It was a gentle hand and ringless. She said, "My name is Jennifer Garvey."

I held my face expressionless. I'd have to be damned careful here. Jennifer Garvey was saying, "My husband was Carl Garvey, the writer. Have you heard of him?"

I said, "Uhh-h-h-h, yes, of course. Wasn't his last book published recently?"

"That's right. *Monastery Nightmare* and it's going great guns, better than any of his previous stories. Also, it's causing a certain amount of conjecture which I find to be extremely uncomfortable."

"How's that, Mrs. Garvey?"

"Well, you see, Carl has been believed dead for nearly a year. His sailboat was found abandoned on Lake Michigan. He'd had a heart attack several months earlier and the assumption was that another seizure had struck him while he was out on the water."

"It seems logical enough."

"Certainly. At that time there were no other choices."

"And now there are?"

143

Ross H. Spencer

Jennifer Garvey searched my face with puzzled blue eyes. She said, "Yes, Mr. Lassiter, suddenly there is a question that cries out for an answer."

"And that would be?"

She put a tiny blue-enameled lighter to a cork-tipped cigarette and permitted smoke to trickle from her finely chiseled nostrils. "Was *Monastery Nightmare* written prior to Carl's death or is he alive somewhere?"

I fumbled in my desk drawer and found a fresh pack of Marlboros. I said, "Do you believe that Carl Garvey wrote the book?"

She snapped her lighter vexedly and held it to my cigarette. "I don't know *what* to think! The style would appear to be Carl's but I'm not an authority on the Hillary Condor series. Quite frankly, it struck me as being terribly contrived nonsense and I've read precious little of it."

"What you seem to be saying is that your husband may have faked this tragedy. It wouldn't have been too difficult."

"Well, it certainly falls within the realm of possibility. But if he *is* dead and if he *didn't* write *Monastery Nightmare*, then, for heaven's sake, who *did*?"

I stepped around it. "Was there a will?"

"Yes, and I'm Carl's heir, but in his will the Hillary Condor books are referred to individually, not as a group."

"And this could throw *Monastery Nightmare* up for grabs."

"I'm afraid it could."

"There's serious money involved?"

"God, yes! I've heard that the movie rights may go for more than a million dollars."

"Where did you hear that?"

"It's just grapevine but it's fairly reliable grapevine."

I felt like a sheep-killing dog in this role. I said, "How would you describe your relationship with Mr. Garvey?"

Jennifer Garvey licked her rosy lips and stared at the small blue handbag in her lap. She cleared her throat and uncrossed her legs, affording me a glimpse of smooth, tawny thigh. She wasn't wearing panty hose, the nemesis of impromptu sex. She said, "We were cordial for the most part. We were mentally compatible and we had downright scintillating conversation. We

MONASTERY NIGHTMARE

shared an appreciation of a great many things and we laughed a lot. Does that answer your question?"

"Yes. Physically it was a bust."

"Mr. Lassiter, you must understand that there were some twenty years separating us. I had certain natural hungers that Carl was utterly incapable of satisfying."

"And you found relief in other quarters?"

Jennifer Garvey looked up, her blue eyes plumbing the depths of mine. "Does this shock you?"

"Not at all. I've been around the block a couple of times. Was your husband aware of your activities?"

She shook her head. "No, I was very discreet." She thought about it. "But Carl may have sensed something. Do you know what I mean?"

"I've been married, Mrs. Garvey."

She glanced at her watch, a delicate, dime-size wafer on her golden arm. She said, "Mr. Lassiter, this visit was made merely to establish your availability. I must meet with Carl's attorney this afternoon and there isn't time to accommodate further discussion just now. Would you consider helping me in this matter?"

"I'd be glad to do what I can."

"Then if I could persuade you to have dinner with me this evening we'd be able to talk at length."

"My pleasure."

She stood and so did I. She smoothed her white skirt over trim, tight buttocks. She said, "Sarno's at six-thirty? In the lounge?"

She smiled and it was like she'd flipped on a battery of floodlights. I watched her go out. My God, what a hunk of female! And she was hurting. I could feel it.

145

49

*T*he drab afternoon wore listlessly on. I dug a can of Stroh's out of my beat-up office refrigerator and stood at the office window, looking down into Adams Street. Hardly an exhilarating sight. A carbon copy of any other metropolis route. Grimy, gritty gray. Swarming but lifeless. There were no people down there, just hordes of tight-faced big-city robots going through their programmed motions. Yesterday, today and tomorrow, running down, wearing out, replaced by more from the assembly line. Well, I was in no position to criticize their parade. I belonged in the damn thing, right out in front, carrying a colorless banner. No place to go, nothing to do when I got there and no way to get back. Operating a Donald Duck detective agency, hitting the hay with the wife of a prominent evangelist, living with the daughter of a Mafia honcho and involved in a Keystone Kops caper with an ancient female Don Quixote and her research-happy sidekick. No gold stars there.

But *Monastery Nightmare* could alter my life. It could send Crystal and me to Suva Point where our son would grow up with a British accent, look for *jig-jig* and play rugby. Well, there was nothing wrong with a bit of *jig-jig*, I'd chased it for twenty-five years, and rugby was a better game than American football. However, I hadn't seen the money yet and Suva Point was one helluva distance from Chicago, Illinois. There's many a slip 'twixt cup and lip. Shakespeare? Damned if I knew. I'd have to ask my typist.

So back to the ball game. I wondered what had prompted Jennifer Garvey to visit my hole-in-the-wall agency. The yellow

MONASTERY NIGHTMARE

pages, in all probability. I ran a fair-sized ad, not as big as Buck Westerville's but it caught the eye. Buck's spread was twice the size of mine and so were his rates. She hadn't visited Buck, that was certain, because he'd have hooked her on the spot. His sales spiel was polished, his business quarters were impressive and he had a secretary-receptionist.

I killed my can of beer, got another, and considered Mrs. Garvey. A downright steamy number, no other way to read her. Pamela Frost had described her as a full-blown little tart. She might be. She really hadn't needed to hit me over the head with it. She could have tiptoed around the matter. When a woman looks a complete stranger in the eye and announces that she has strolled the primrose path, she is, in effect, declaring herself to be fair game. She's making no promises but she's saying try me, you'll never be sure until you do. And I just might do that. I wasn't married *yet*.

I locked up and walked over to State Street, then north to Randolph. That put me just a half block from Sarno's. I'd catch the biggest piece of the happy hour. All drinks half-price, four till six. Half-price, half-strength, but there wasn't much they could do to bottled beer.

50

*T*he bar at Sarno's was full. So were the booths and all of those teetery, little two-person tables. The crowd was typically 5:00 P.M. Loop. Graying executives on the make for tender young secretaries. Graying secretaries on the make for tender young executives. Piped in music and the steady buzz of voices and the jingle of cash registers and cigarette smoke and shrill female laughter and loud perfume and all the handshaking and false exuberance that could be stuffed into a low-ceilinged forty-by-forty room. The man working my end of the bar was a dour, fat guy named Barney Critz and I'd known him since he'd been night manager at the Kangaroo Klub on Wabash Avenue. He said, "Bottle of Stroh's, Luke?" I nodded and Barney brought the beer. He pushed my money away and said, "Every day about this time I get an urge to puke."

I said, "With all this sweet young stuff waltzing around under your nose?"

Barney Critz snorted. "Sweet young stuff? Luke, there ain't one of these bimbos what couldn't screw the peaches off a Rocky Mountain goat."

A gray-haired guy on my right had put away his share. He hiccuped, burped, polished off his double martini and hit the road. Five seconds later Jennifer Garvey popped nimbly into the vacant seat. She checked her watch and said, "We're early, aren't we?"

I said, "I ran out of beer at the office."

She turned on her high-voltage smile. She said, "I don't have an excuse. I just . . . came early." I liked her voice. Slightly

MONASTERY NIGHTMARE

coarse, like honey beginning to turn to sugar. She spun her barstool and faced me. "Mr. Lassiter, I want you to meet Jonas Solomon. Solly's handled Carl's affairs for years and you may need his cooperation."

A tall, curly-headed guy of something like forty was standing directly behind me. He had canny green eyes, a slightly hooked nose and a jutting clefted jaw. He was impeccably attired in a three-hundred-dollar Clausen Brothers gray gabardine leisure suit and a pale-lime silk sports shirt open at the neck. Studiedly casual. He wore a thick-linked gold necklace with a Krugerrand attached and I didn't like him. I just didn't like the sonofabitch and it wasn't because Pamela Frost had intimated that he was crooked. It was because I have an instant distrust for men who wear necklaces. When they're around I keep my legs tightly crossed. Necklaces are for females. I'd even resented dog tags. I shook hands with Jonas Solomon. For a guy wearing a necklace he had a pretty fair grip. I said, "Call me Luke."

He said, "Luke it is. I'm Solly." The hell he was. He'd be Solomon to me. He smiled and squeezed my shoulder. I'm not particularly wild about shoulder-squeezers either. He said, "We'll have to talk. Lunch at the Hong Kong Room tomorrow? My treat." Strike three. I don't like people who say "my treat." They come on as condescending, like you're eight years old and they're popping for an ice cream cone. In Hubbard, Ohio, they'd said "It's on me" and you took it or left it.

I said, "Okay, Solomon, it's on you."

He excused himself. "Simply must dash. Terribly pressing engagement. Redhead." He didn't say which sex. He squeezed my shoulder again and headed for the exit.

Jennifer Garvey was eyeing my beer. She said, "I think I'll have one of those. I'm parched." I waved until I caught the baleful eye of Barney Critz. I pointed to my bottle and then to Jennifer. He came with the beer, poured a half-glass and Jennifer drank thirstily. She licked the foam from her upper lip with a pink and delicately deliberate tongue, watching me with steady blue eyes. She said, "I made dining room reservations for eight o'clock. Will that be all right?"

"No great hurry. Tell me more about *Monastery Nightmare*. Who submitted it to Wellington Books?"

149

ROSS H. SPENCER

"I don't know. I was never consulted and neither was Solly."

"Did your husband have a literary agent?"

"Yes, a Pamela Frost on Monroe Street but they had no long-term contract. They took it book by book. She never heard of *Monastery Nightmare* until it was in the bookstores. Wellington Books won't reveal the source so there's something fishy there. Normally they'd refer inquiries to *some*body."

"You've contacted the publisher?"

"Yes. Wellington simply notes that this is a business matter of an extremely confidential nature."

"Solomon can't budge them?"

"Not without a legal battle. Do you have the slightest idea how long it would take to get this matter into a court of law? Are you familiar with the delaying maneuvers available to a publishing house of Wellington's prestige and power?"

"I'm sure it could get sticky."

"It could get so sticky that the money would be in somebody's Swiss account long before Wellington ran out of postponements."

"Where would you suggest that I look for your husband?"

"He was a sailing fanatic. You might nose around the lakefront. He drank in some of the little places in our neighborhood but I don't believe anyone knew he was a writer. I don't expect you to pick him off a tree. Carl was clever and if he's alive and hiding he'll be difficult to find."

"I don't like to discourage you but it's a hundred-to-one he's dead."

"I know that but it boils down to leaving no stone unturned."

"What sort of fellow was he? Moody? Bad-tempered?"

"Hardly ever. He was a loner essentially and all the more so when he was writing. When he wrote he drank a great deal. He told me that alcohol served to short-circuit the inhibitory panels of his mind, that it enabled him to grant audience to thoughts he'd have barred when sober."

"Look, if Garvey decided to run away from it all was there another woman to run to?"

Jennifer Garvey smiled sadly. "Mr. Lassiter, Carl wasn't the world's greatest lover."

"I'm not talking about making love. I'm talking about the

150

MONASTERY NIGHTMARE

understanding that men seek and sometimes find away from home."

"I don't believe there was anyone else. To the best of my knowledge Pamela Frost was his only other close female acquaintance. I'm certain that their years of association produced some time in bed but people change. Pamela let herself go to hell. She's hog-fat. Furthermore she's blind. Carl was virtually impotent. I'd be shocked if their more recent relationship had to do with anything other than Carl's writing."

I motioned to Barney Critz for another round. I said, "Still thirsty?"

"Oh, yes. And getting hungry. Very, very hungry."

We locked gazes and there was a current between us that you could have hung the week's wash on. I said, "We aren't even drunk yet."

She smiled the faintest of smiles. She said, "Do we have to be drunk?"

I said, "I doubt it. It's more custom than anything, don't you think?"

She nodded slowly, holding my eyes with hers. "Are we talking about the same thing?"

I said, "Probably."

For the better part of a minute we sparred with glances, saying nothing. Barney brought our fresh beers and she watched him pour them. She picked up her glass and her hand was trembling perceptibly. She gulped some of the beer, swallowing very hard. Then her hand fell to my knee, still shaking, and she averted her eyes. She said, "Oh, God!"

I said, "I know."

"Do you?"

"I think so."

She pushed her glass back and forth on the wood-grained Formica bar-top. She sighed. "My move?"

"Your move."

"To hell with dinner?"

"To hell with dinner."

Jennifer Garvey drove an Italian sports car.

Just like the newspapers said.

151

51

I let myself into the office and slouched in my swivel chair. My ass was dragging and my phone was ringing. Crystal said, "Luke, where have you been?" Not Gestapo-style. There was concern in her voice.

I said, "On a case."

"The whole damn *night*?"

"Certainly, the whole damn night. That's part of my ball game."

"Some ball game."

"It's the only game in town."

"You must be tired."

"Baby, you have no idea."

"Then close up and come home. You need sleep. Sleep that knits up the ravelled sleeve of care, balm of hurt minds, great nature's second course, chief nourisher in life's feast."

"*Macbeth.*"

"How did you know?"

"We went to high school together."

"Come on home and I'll put you to sleep."

"I'll sleep tonight."

"Yes, but by then you'll be too pooped to pop."

"I'm already too pooped to pop."

"Luke?"

"Yeah?"

Crystal giggled. She said, "Try licorice. It's an aphrodisiac."

52

Jonas Solomon met me at the reception desk of the Hong Kong Room, the characteristic Chinese restaurant with bead curtains in its doorways, needlework dragons on its walls and little red-shaded lamps all over the place. Solomon was togged out in a maroon blazer with a large white S on its pocket, white silk shirt, white slacks and white suede shoes. I didn't get a look at his socks but I'd have bet a case of Stroh's that they were maroon. He wore a silver necklace from which swung a maroon-enameled mermaid. With white eyes. Honest to God. Solomon squeezed my shoulder and led me to his booth. He said, "Drink?"

I said, "Frequently."

Our order was taken by a nicely put together Chinese girl in a slinky, floor-length black dress with a peacock embroidered over the left breast and the skirt slit all the way up to her rib cage. I had a vodka martini on the rocks with an anchovy-stuffed olive. Solomon had a sweet whiskey-sour straight-up with a slice of orange and a maraschino cherry. It figured. He slumped into a corner of the booth and said, "Well, Luke, what can I tell you that might be of help?"

I said, "Why don't you start with Pamela Frost?"

He nodded. "A nice lady. Perhaps a bit heavy-handed but very capable. She raised Carl Garvey from a literary pup and she led him through the publishing jungle, so to speak. Pamela's probably the best of Chicago's literary agents."

"How good is that?"

Solomon made a deprecatory limp-wristed gesture. "Not so

ROSS H. SPENCER

very. Chicago doesn't have many and the hotshots are in New York. Better access to publishing houses."

"Were she and Garvey lovers at one time?"

"Oh, I believe it's fairly common knowledge that they had something cooking before Pam got fat. Have you ever noticed that fat women do strange things?"

"Yes, but I believe that's a tendency carried over from when they were skinny. What was so strange about Pamela Frost?"

"I don't know exactly but Carl used to say that he thought she was coming apart at the seams. Might have been menopause. Don't quote me."

"*Monastery Nightmare* has really scrambled the eggs, hasn't it?"

"Definitely. It has a lot of people running in tight little circles."

"What's your opinion, Solomon? Could Garvey be alive and, if so, why would he be playing a game like this?"

Solomon munched thoughtfully on his maraschino cherry. "Anything's possible. As to what he'd be up to I couldn't begin to guess. Carl Garvey had a peculiar and subtle mind."

"Had he exhibited any signs of cracking up? A couple dozen books must have taken something out of him."

"None that I could detect. It wouldn't have been the writing, anyway. That came easily enough to Carl. There may have been other pressures." He shifted his gaze to one of the needlework dragons on the wall. "Jennifer would be the one to ask. Have you seen her condominium?"

I deadpanned it. "Is there a reason I should have?"

"Well, Luke, almost everybody has. Jennifer's a nympho, you know."

"Oh?"

"She doesn't mince words about it, not when you get to know her well. There'd be no point in it. But she's a fine person, her nymphomania notwithstanding."

I swirled the ice in my martini glass. I said, "Some of my best friends are nymphomaniacs."

53

I hadn't seen Jake Perry since we'd met down in the lobby in July. Now he was in my office, sitting in my wooden chair, pushing his hat back, taking a cigarette from my pack on the desk and saying, "You oughta get that goddam elevator fixed."

I said, "I keep asking 'em and they keep telling me wait, everything's gonna be just dandy."

"What'll you bet George Halas don't own this roach ranch? The tactics are identical. Wait, wait, wait."

"Still on midnights, Jake?"

"Days now. Luke, yesterday you had lunch with an attorney named Jonas Solomon."

"You here in an official capacity?"

"Sure am. You had lunch with this lawyer yesterday."

"Did I?"

"That's what his secretary says."

"Okay, so I had lunch with him."

"What did you two talk about?"

"Jake, you know I can't go into that."

Jake sighed an Oh-Jesus-Christ sigh. He said, "Luke, Jonas Solomon was gunned down in his apartment last night."

"I see."

"Well, you goddam well *better* see! What did you talk about?"

"Who shot him?"

Jake rolled his eyes. "Luke, if I knew that I wouldn't be up here."

"Well, it wasn't anything that would have gotten him killed."

155

Jake Perry's frown was silently ominous. I said, "Okay, I'm looking for a guy. I thought Solomon might throw some light on the matter."

"Did he?"

"No."

"Who's the man you're looking for?"

"One of Solomon's former clients. A writer named Garvey."

"Carl Garvey? The guy who disappeared from his boat last fall?"

"The same."

"You think maybe he didn't really fall off the boat?"

"Not me. My clients."

"That's plural?"

"Yes. As in more than one."

"Who are your clients?"

"I can't tell you that, Jake."

"Okay, skip that one. How well did you know Solomon?"

"Hardly at all. Met him night before last, had lunch with him yesterday. That was it."

"You knew he was gay?"

"I assumed as much. He wore necklaces."

Jake nodded. "He had a drawerful." He stood up. "All right, Luke, thanks. How's business?"

I shrugged. "So-so."

"Hang in there."

"Trying like hell."

"If you think of anything let me know."

"Sure, Jake."

He went out. He was a very dedicated cop. Some of them get that way. Even in Chicago.

54

I called Buck Westerville. I said, "Garvey's attorney was scragged last night."

"Jonas Solomon?"

"You knew him?"

"I've heard of him. I must have missed it in the papers. How did you find out?"

"A cop told me."

"How was he killed?"

"Shot."

"Where?"

"Hell, I don't know. Probably in the chest."

"I mean *where*?"

"In his apartment."

"Who was the cop?"

"Homicide bull. Jake Perry."

"Jake Perry. Yeah, tough cookie. Why did Perry contact you?"

"I had lunch with Solomon yesterday."

"Why?"

"You told me to do the things I'd do if I was really looking for Carl Garvey. That's one of the things I'd have done."

There was a long pause. Then Buck said, "Well, Luke, let's get something straight here. In the event that Empire State Casualty has someone checking on this thing locally I want it known that you're looking around but I didn't mean for you to tear up the goddam woodwork. Give me the old standard investigation but

157

don't *dig*. We can't afford to have you involved in a murder. Christ, there's no predicting what that could lead to!"

"I'm not involved in a murder. I had lunch with a guy. Chicken chow mein."

"I know, but play it cool. You aren't *really* looking for Carl Garvey, get that through your head."

"Okay."

"Solomon have anything to say?"

"He squeezed my shoulder."

"All right, Luke, make it look good but let it go at that. My God, the next thing I know you'll be sleeping with Garvey's widow!"

55

*P*amela Frost was a wonder in her kitchen. Following vodka martinis and small talk there'd been porterhouse steaks, fries, salads, pound cake with cherry sauce and black coffee laced with excellent brandy. Now we sat on an immense sofa, sipping our coffee and brandy, smoking and listening to a subdued tape of Dixieland blues featuring an excellent trombone. Georg Brunis, I'd have bet on it, but I didn't ask. The apartment was sumptuous, its living room paneled in wormwood, carpeted in ankle-deep beige and brightened by draperies of vivid hues and the dust covers of hundreds of books in recessed casings. I said, "You amaze me."

"How so?"

"The cooking. How can you do it?"

"Keeping strict order is the secret. You've heard of chess players who play the game blindfolded. It's a matter of remembering where you've left things. That knack comes to blind people. It isn't at all unusual. Let's not talk about me. Let's talk about you."

"Let's talk about *Monastery Nightmare*. You haven't mentioned it."

She bit her lower lip. "I'd rather not discuss it, Luke. I'm not at all certain that Carl wrote the book but, if he's alive and writing, his submission of it through other channels was a poor display of gratitude. I put Carl Garvey on the map."

"Have you had it read to you?"

"Yes, and I enjoyed it. It has the old Garvey ring, a feeling of authenticity."

159

"Then you think that Garvey may have written it?"

"Let's just say that if it wasn't Carl it was a close student of the Garvey technique, a capable writer adapting himself to the Garvey outlook and doing a downright terrific job. A writer such as yourself, perhaps."

"I'm not much of a writer."

"I'm speaking of potential. My neighbor read a few of your short stories to me the other evening. All you need is a character of your own. I liked the one in 'Devilbird,' that one-legged detective."

"Casey Carruthers?"

"Yes, the one with the sawed-off shotgun embedded in his wooden leg. He has strong possibilities and you could do a series on him but you'll need help in converting from short stories to novels."

"I'd hoped to do something better, something with depth."

"That would come. You'd just be serving an apprenticeship with Casey Carruthers."

I finished my coffee and brandy and Pam said, "Another?"

I said, "Yes, please. How did you know I was dry?"

She said, "Your cup has clinked into your saucer a dozen times. If it isn't empty it can't be far from it."

Over the new coffee and brandy she said, "Luke, tell me, are you serious about the Fiji Islands or is that just so much chatter?"

"At the moment it's chatter."

"But you'd really like to live there? Get away from it all and write?"

"I would, yes, very much."

"I'm going to keep that in mind."

The tape ran out and there was silence in the room. Then, suddenly, she crushed her cigarette into an ashtray and said, "Aren't we at that time of evening when gentlemen invite ladies to bed?" She smiled her hungry, toothy smile and gripped my arm.

I shrugged.

That was a mistake.

56

*P*amela Frost was like a mama polar bear that has polished off a barrel of Spanish fly. Before she left the couch she was as naked as a jaybird. By the time we reached the bedroom door so was I. She tore the buttons off my shirt and busted the zipper of my fly. She removed her dark glasses and threw a flying block into me. We hit the bed with me on the bottom and I stayed there. She swayed, rolled, bucked, bounced, lunged, moaned, groaned, shivered, quivered, wiggled, jiggled and giggled. Then she got down to business. In the darkness her gray eyes shone like foxfire. She roared like a lion and howled like a broken-hearted timber wolf. Late in the Sexual Olympics the bed caved in and we crashed to the floor. Pamela Frost paid no attention. She cussed and gasped and recited poetry. She sang one chorus of "Fascination" and two of "Down in Jungle Town." She scratched, bit and kicked and by three in the morning I was afraid she was going to kill me. By four-thirty I was certain of it. At last she said, "You'll have to excuse me. I got carried away."

I said, "I wasn't far from it myself."

She said, "There are times when I become quite passionate."

I said, "Really?"

She said, "What are you doing tonight?"

I licked my bruised lips and put my fingers to the large lumps on my forehead. I said, "That would depend on what they tell me in intensive care."

I stumbled down the stairs and into the glorious freedom of a damp, gray dawn. I found my car and fumbled for my keys. A squad car pulled up. A cop leaned out and said, "Where you headed, buddy?"

I said, "Australia."

He shone a light on me and whistled. "Bad night?"

"I've had better."

"Mugged?"

"You're close."

"Must have been a tough bunch."

"She sure was."

I drove home and climbed the stairs on wobbly legs. Crystal was waiting for me. She said, "Oh, sweet Jesus!"

I said, "I believe that just about covers it."

She said, "I knew you should have turned Catholic."

I said, "Don't blame Itchy. I fell down the elevator shaft."

I staggered into the bathroom and started hot water running in the tub. I gazed thoughtfully into the mirror. My nose was out of line and one of my eyebrows was missing. I undressed and lowered myself into the water. I laid back and let the heat soothe my aching, abused body. I wondered how the hell Carl Garvey had managed to handle the sexual blitzkriegs of Pamela Frost. Next to Itchy Balzino she was the strongest human being I'd ever encountered.

I dozed off and awakened to Crystal tapping me on the shoulder. She said, "For God's sake get out of there! You'll freeze to death!" The water had gone icy cold and my teeth rattled like a Latin rhythm section. I piled out of the tub and toweled myself until my blood resumed the circulatory process. Crystal leaned against the sink, watching me with bloodshot eyes. I said, "Have you been crying?"

"No, I've been up all night."

"Waiting for me?"

"Yes, and reading *Monastery Nightmare* again. Luke, that little poem at the beginning, the one about reading but reading not too well. Does that have something to do with the Professor James nuclear formula?"

"I'll explain it when we get to Suva Point."

"Where's Suva Point?"

"A little southwest of here."

"Luke, let's go to bed."

MONASTERY NIGHTMARE

"Aw, Crystal, have a heart!"

"Don't get all excited! I mean just to sleep. You're tired and I like to hold you when you sleep."

Crystal put me to bed. She held me and I started to float away. It was a warm, secure, delicious sensation. I thought of a title for a book: *Love Carries a Licorice Luger*.

Carl Garvey might have liked that one.

57

Stash Dubinski called me right in the middle of my morning pecan roll. He said, "Luke, can you round up the sunshine girls for tonight? Lennie's boys will be pulling the old rain gutters off of Leffingwell this afternoon."

"Will they have that bathtub hoist arrangement ready to go?"

"It'll be all set and I'll get the water in that top tub before I check out this evening. For Christ's sake, Luke, be careful!"

"Thanks, Stash. This'll be the end of it."

"You better believe this'll be the end of it! You jazz around with Lady Luck long enough and she kicks you right in the balls!"

"Shakespeare?"

"Dubinski."

I called Barb and she rang me back in half an hour. "Okay, Luke, it's on for tonight. Candy can't make it but Elizabeth and Geraldine are available."

"What's with the Stoneman chick?"

"She wants to see her guy."

"Fine. Too many cooks spoil the broth."

The day passed uneventfully until Johnny Huskin called just as I was getting ready to close up. He said, "This Lassiter?"

"Hisself."

The smile in Huskin's voice was brief. He said, "Looky, Lassiter, my wife's writin' club got some kind of special doin's tonight an' I was won'drin' iffen mebbe y'all might drop out an' visit me. We could sit aroun' an' have us a cracker-barrel session."

MONASTERY NIGHTMARE

I said, "Reverend, if it's about my getting religion I don't feel that I lean too strongly in that direction."

"Naw, nothin' lak that. Y'all a good ole country boy an' a pleasin' feller to talk to. Y'all doan gotta be no Christian to 'preciate down-home-style conversation." His vast loneliness spilled from the receiver. He was a stray dog, the one you just can't walk away from.

I said, "I can come but I won't be able to stay long. I have an important appointment late this evening."

"Wall, shucks, so do I. Only a hour would fix me up juss fine. It's gonna be good to talk with a man what speaks my language. How's lak seven o'clock? I'll keep a eye peeled."

"That's a country line. My father was always keeping an eye peeled."

Huskin chuckled. He said, "Lassiter, they gits things said in th' country. Couple ole country boys kin say more in ten minutes than a wagonload of Harvard professors kin say in a week."

"See you, Reverend." I hung up. Huskin was dead right about country boys but he was dead wrong about me. I was the worm in his apple and he didn't know it. But he knew that his apple was rotten.

I made it out to White Birch Knolls a little after seven and Huskin said, "Pity y'all couldn't meet my wife. She left fer that club shindig mebbe twenny minutes ago."

"Some other time."

Huskin showed me through the house. Magnificent would have been a feeble word. In the living room was a white stone fireplace in which you could have barbecued a bull elephant. The walls were of carved oak paneling and the sculptured shag carpeting must have cost upwards of forty bucks a yard. Over the fireplace there was a gigantic oil painting. Johnny Huskin shaking hands with Jesus Christ. Both were smiling and Christ's left hand rested affectionately on Huskin's right shoulder. I stood, just staring, and Huskin said, "That there feller's a friend of mine. He died fer me an' I been tryin' to make it up to Him one way or th' other."

"I haven't met him."

"Oh, y'all doan got to worry none 'bout that, He gonna be comin' 'roun' your way. Wunna these here days y'all gonna look

165

up an' there He gonna be, juss stannin' with His lovin' arms outstretched, sayin', 'Come on home, ole boy.' Y'all know where I run into Him?"

"I can't imagine."

"In Clendennon's Pool Hall down by th' switch yard in Gatlinburg, Tennessee, that's where. I was bankin' th' nine-ball 'cross-side when He showed up. He said, 'Drop that there cue stick, sonny boy, reckon it's high time y'all done straightened up an' started actin' lak a man.'"

"Just like that?"

"Yep, juss lak that, an' y'all know what I done?"

"Well, I don't know about you but I'd have blown the nine-ball."

"Hey, I juss throwed down my cigarette an' I left my bottle of beer an' I stomped out of that there crummy ole pool hall walkin' tall an' I ain't never been back since."

"What happened to the nine-ball?"

"It went in lak it had eyes." Huskin sat on the bench of a black piano that must have been brought in on a flatcar. He said, "Here's a li'l ditty what says it all fer me." He sang it.

> *"Jesus, Jesus, Jesus,*
> *Sweetest name I know.*
> *Fills my every longin',*
> *Keeps me singin' as I go."*

It took me back and I said, "I remember that one!"

"Wall, then come on an' bust in with me!" He sang it twice and I joined him. He looked up smiling. "Y'all sings fine harmony, Lassiter. Means y'all a good feller at heart. Harmony comes straight from th' gizzard. Never knowed no real bad fokes what could sing harmony worth a plugged nickel."

I said, "My parents were First Church of God people." I grinned. "They didn't believe in the Millennium or speaking in tongues."

Huskin grinned back. "Wall, 'course they was plumb wrong but they was good fokes anyways." I didn't know what it was with Huskin and me. We were miles apart but we liked each

MONASTERY NIGHTMARE

other. It was a chemical thing. He left his piano bench and said, "Lassiter, what y'all think of this here place?"

"It's beautiful."

"Wall, y'see, there's th' differ'nce 'twixt y'all an' me. I doan lak it no-how. I'd druther be back in Tennessee an', Good Lord willin', thass ezzackly where I gonna be 'fore too much longer." He led me into the dining room where I saw a table that could have accommodated the 37th Infantry Division on review. On the wall were displayed dozens of firearms. I studied the impressive array and saw virtually everything but a Gatling gun.

I said, "You have any use for this arsenal?"

Huskin said, "It's juss a hobby. I never mess with it but I kin shoot th' moustache offen a grasshopper at a hunnert yards, doan you never doubt it. Learnt how to shoot whilst I was a young'un. My daddy done taught me. Times was tough an' we needed meat fer th' table."

I said, "Quite a collection. A man could stand off a regiment."

"Yeah, reckon so, but th' only way I'd ever pull one of them there triggers is in defense of my wife an' home. Thass when I'd shoot first an' ask questions later. God give me my wife an' He put this here roof over our heads an' I figger He wants me to keep 'em safe an' soun'."

Somehow I doubted that Huskin would shoot if he was surrounded by werewolves. He'd heard that sort of talk around the potbellied stove in a Tennessee general store and he was quoting it from memory much as he quoted scripture. The ability to kill comes with fear or insanity and I saw neither in Johnny Huskin. He was a good and gentle man of a caliber you seldom meet.

He said, "Lassiter, I hates bein' cooped up in th' house any longer'n necessary. I got me a ole holler log out in th' woods where I does me some thinkin' an' prayin'. It's my private altar, kind of. Less you an' me walk out thataway an' sit a while."

"No sermons, Reverend?"

"No sermons, Lassiter. Iffen God wants to talk to y'all He gonna do it at His own time in His own way."

Huskin's hollow log had no bark and there were patches of moss at either end. When we sat down he said, "There's somethin' 'bout a ole holler log a body never pays much mind to."

167

ROSS H. SPENCER

"He'll pay some mind if you're talking about black ants."

"No, that ain't it but it'd take a country boy to know 'bout black ants. Y'see, holler logs ain't here by no accident. There juss gotta be a holler log ever' so offen in any ole woods on account of thass how God got th' whole business put together. Holler logs is refuge an' God leaves 'em aroun' fer th' helpless critters what doan got no way left to turn, lak mebbe a mama rabbit with some big ole hairy dog juss a-snappin' at her rear end. It's lak th' Christian experience, Lassiter. Th' Christian experience is a holler log fer th' troubled soul."

I turned to look at him. I said, "Reverend, I think it's *your* soul that's troubled tonight. If it wasn't, you wouldn't have called me out here."

Huskin sat on the log, twisting at a twig he'd picked up, staring glumly at the forest floor. He said, "Wall, it ain't ezzackly my soul what's actin' up so much as it's my mind. I got me a feelin' my wife is drawin' away from me."

"You care deeply for her, don't you?"

Huskin snapped the twig and threw it away. He said, "Lassiter, in all my born days there ain't never been but two wimmen I rilly ever give a hoot fer. 'Course I loves ever'body in th' Christian way, y'all unnerstan', but my mother an' Barbara is th' onliest females what ever got to my heart. Why, Lassiter, I fell in love with Barb soon's I seen her an' there ain't never been no change." He found another twig and studied it. " 'Course I done made me some mistakes along life's road juss lak th' rest of us." His smile was sad. "Even preachers makes mistakes. There is times when we juss ain't nowheres near so strong as Th' Good Lord had in mind fer us to be."

I made no comment and Huskin continued. "I reckon I knows what's at th' root of our troubles. It's th' big city, Lassiter, thass what it is. Barb's from a one-hoss burg juss outside Duluth an' I'm from down Gatlinburg way an' I figger we misses them wide open spaces where a feller kin git hisself a breath of fresh air ever' so offen."

"You're really going back to Tennessee?"

"I been plannin' on it real serious-like. Gonna scratch all them meetin's an' all them telecasts an' head south." The moon was coming up and early evening stars glimmered through the

168

MONASTERY NIGHTMARE

leaves and Huskin caught me looking upward. He said, "Lassiter, you ain't never rilly seen no stars till you gits down Tennessee way. Why, man, in Tennessee we got us stars bigger'n *base*balls!"

I said, "Reverend Huskin, you're just plain, flat-out homesick."

"Yeah, I got to git us away from all this here Chicago-style carryin' on. There's things we gotta leave behind us an' go home an' start all over agin. Feller needs a fresh beginnin' now an' then. Y'all ever think of hoein' a new row, Lassiter?"

"Oh, yes. Often."

"Recently?"

"Recently? Since I was born."

"Then you oughta do it."

"I've done it. Every row's the same. Rocks. You plant rocks, you grow rocks."

"Well, Lassiter, I cain't speak fer you but I've worked pow'ful hard over th' years. My evangelistic association done already contributed more'n fifty million dollars to needy fokes all over this here globe. I walks into a shoe store an' twenny people wants my autygraph but my own wife won't hardly even speak to me. I'm gonna sell this here place an' give most of what I git to charity. I gonna keep me juss enough to carry us back to Tennessee an' buy us a few acres. I gonna build me a li'l ole white house in th' back an' a li'l ole white church up front an' I gonna toil fer Th' Lord same like always only I gonna have me a lot more time fer Barbara. Juss ain't no tellin', we might even git aroun' to havin' us a baby. Shucks, we ain't too old yet!"

"Reverend, I wish you all the luck in the world." I'd never spoken more sincere words in my life.

Huskin snorted. "It ain't never luck, Lassiter, it's *God*! Ain't nothin' gonna happen no way to nobody nowheres iffen it doan got God's okay stamped on it."

I shrugged. I said, "Well, whatever. I just hope it works out for you."

Huskin stood. He said, "Lassiter, I sho' 'preciates y'all drivin' clean out here to keep me comp'ny. Been a real pleasure talkin' to y'all." The previous autumn's leaves crackled under our feet as we walked toward my car. The trees rustled in a warm wind

169

ROSS H. SPENCER

that had sprung out of the west. Rain was on the way. We spooked a rabbit and Huskin laughed. He said, "Y'all know where that there rabbit's headed?"

"The hollow log?"

"No place else!" When we reached my car he grabbed my hand and he really clamped down on it. "Wall, thanks, Lassiter. We got to do this agin sometime!"

"Sure thing, Reverend."

I couldn't get out of there fast enough. I was doing sixty-five before I reached Old Brasham Road.

58

*I*t was 8:15 and I had some time to kill before I rendezvoused with Barbara Huskin. I stopped at Griswold's Bar and Liquors and I was talking with Sam Blake when I heard rain on the roof. It developed into a deluge and it lasted for more than an hour. Then, almost instantly, it was over, like someone had thrown a great master switch, and I left Griswold's to head south on 294. The wind had dropped off to a whisper and the September moon hung up there big and bright and all alone. One last ragged black cloud remnant drifted reluctantly toward forever. It occurred to me that I'd never see that particular cloud again and the knowledge was strangely saddening. I wondered where clouds go to die.

Barb picked me up at my apartment and she was driving to Elizabeth Fudge's place when I said, "Your telephone isn't bugged. If it was bugged your husband would have nailed me tonight."

"Why? Did he call you?"

"Yes, and I drove out to see him. He invited me."

"Is he suspicious again?"

"I went out there thinking that he might be but he wasn't."

"Then what did he want?"

"Someone to talk to. He's lonely, Barb. He's the loneliest sonofabitch I've ever met."

"He's the best damned actor you've ever met."

"Not Huskin. He's as straight as a string and he loves hell out of you."

"Johnny Huskin loves hell out of Johnny Huskin. Did you see

171

that utterly ridiculous painting over the fireplace? Didn't that tell you something?"

"Something, yes, but not everything. Barb, why don't you give him a child, something he can focus on?"

"Because I'm over thirty, that's why! Because thirty-year-old mothers get all sprung out of shape."

"You'd be doing something for him."

"I've already done something for him. I've given him eleven years of my life."

"You could have had kids earlier."

"We couldn't *afford* kids, not at the right time in life. What's this all about, Luke? Was Johnny blubbering on your shoulder?"

"Not blubbering. We just talked. Huskin likes me for some damn fool reason."

"Oh, that's funny! That's a real riot! Johnny likes the man who's riding his old lady! Leave it to Johnny! You'll be at the altar before you know it!"

"He wants to go back to Tennessee. He thinks that maybe you two can find the handle down there."

Barbara Huskin gripped the Mercedes wheel until her knuckles turned white. She blurted a four-letter word and we peeled rubber getting away from a red traffic signal. Obviously the subject was closed.

By the time we reached the Fudge residence she'd cooled down. She said, "Luke, forgive me for being cross. I'm about to be blackmailed and I'm terribly on edge about tonight. There's something in the air, something bad, can't you feel it?"

I could but I didn't admit it. I said, "Nothing to worry about. It'll be a piece of cake."

"I'm all wound up. I need a few drinks and a good old-fashioned screwing. It's been a thousand years!" I busied myself lighting a cigarette and Barb said, "I left the house at six-thirty and I've just been bumming around. I had a sandwich and a milkshake at a drugstore and I wasn't even hungry. I looked at a couple of book racks, I sat in the car and listened to the radio, any damn thing to pass the time. Something's going to go wrong, Luke. We're going to blow it again!"

"Not a chance. This one's perfect. There'll be no night watchman to deal with this time."

MONASTERY NIGHTMARE

Barb tooted the horn and Elizabeth Fudge and Geraldine Swisher emerged. We drove to Bessie Barnum's Circus Tap and parked in the alley. I saw Stash Dubinski's car. Tonight Stash would be sweating bullets.

We watched the minutes crawl by. It was a replay of our earlier episode, waiting and listening to Geraldine Swisher spout research statistics from the darkness of the backseat. Then we saw Rudy Garson's car leave the Leffingwell parking lot and I said, "Let's go, girls."

We piled out of the Mercedes and crossed 72nd Court, Elizabeth Fudge striding purposefully ahead of us carrying a four-cell flashlight in one hand and William Tell's bow in the other. Tell's quiver of arrows was slung over a bony shoulder and she looked a great deal like an anopheles mosquito en route to a nudist colony. In the parking lot she slowed to permit us to catch up and she said, "Mr. Lassiter, please be so kind as to explain tonight's operation again, this time with concision and clarity, please."

I said, "Well, Bonnie, what happens is you climb into a bathtub and I cut a rope and you ride up to the roof and you go through a skylight and down a ladder and six flights of stairs to the main floor of the south wing where you return the Red Sea Documents and then you reverse the procedure and we take you home." A large percentage of which I greatly doubted.

Elizabeth Fudge nodded curtly. She turned to Geraldine Swisher and held out her hand. She said, "Documents." The way a brain surgeon says, "Scalpel." Swisher produced a large manila envelope and Fudge tucked it into the top of her skirt. We had arrived at Lennie Neurotkowski's strange hoist contraption at the rear of Leffingwell Historical Museum. I checked the bottom tub. Its plug had been pulled and it was dry.

At midnight on the button Elizabeth Fudge knelt for a moment before clambering into her conveyance. The big tub strained eagerly against the length of sturdy rope that secured it to the base of a nearby oak tree. Seven stories above us, at the roofline of the building, another bathtub was silhouetted motionless against the clear night skies. Barb stared apprehensively upward. She said, "Luke, what will that old tub hold?"

I said, "Well, water, of course, but beer would be better."

173

ROSS H. SPENCER

"Be serious. How many gallons?"

"Considerably over two hundred, as I understand it." I took out my pocketknife, opened it and began to saw away at the thick retaining rope. I said, "Ready, Bonnie?"

Elizabeth Fudge's voice was clear and steady. "Ready!"

I said, "Well, don't you think you should sit down and hold on?"

She gave me a withering look. "God will protect me, Mr. Lassiter. You tend to your affairs and I'll tend to mine." Like her or not, the old tarantula had guts.

Barb grabbed my arm. She said, "Luke, if I'm not badly mistaken that tub is dribbling water over its side!"

I'd cut halfway through the rope. I said, "It can't be dribbling water. Stash told me he was going to put in eleven or twelve gallons."

Geraldine Swisher said, "Yes, but we had that torrential rain and the old gutters are gone and with all that water rolling off the roof the tub could be full and if it's full, oh, dear God, it must weigh very close to a ton and—" The tethering rope snapped with the report of a rifle and the upper tub plummeted earthward with a high-pitched whistling sound not unlike that of a descending artillery shell. It buried itself in the rain-softened earth with an impact that could have been felt in Peoria.

Elizabeth Fudge was gone. High above us her four-cell flashlight was a westbound pinpoint of light. Twinkle, twinkle, little star. A moment later a shower of arrows began to clatter from the sky and the arrows were followed by a blinding blizzard of age-yellowed papers. There came a great clanging sound and an explosion of breaking glass.

Geraldine Swisher gasped, "Was that the skylight?"

I said, "No, Geraldine, that was the window of Bessie Barnum's Circus Tap."

We took off on the dead run. On 72nd Court shattered glass was scattered from curb to curb. We arrived at Bessie Barnum's Circus Tap in a dead heat with an Elmwood Park squad car. Out of the car climbed Sergeant O'Shaughnessy, the big guy who'd been working the desk on the night of Elizabeth Fudge's ill-fated patriots' parade, and a tall, white-haired man who wore

174

MONASTERY NIGHTMARE

captain's bars on his epaulets. We followed them into the Circus Tap. There, in a booth near Bessie Barnum's missing window, was Elizabeth Fudge's bathtub and in it sat Elizabeth Fudge, diamonds of broken glass shining in her gray hair. She was shaking her head and as the cobwebs began to clear she said, "Shit!" She meant every word of it, you could tell. Her eyes were returning to focus and eventually she spotted me. She said, "Mr. Lassiter, *you* are *fired!*"

Stash Dubinski was seated at a table, his head in his trembling hands, weeping softly. Bessie Barnum stood ankle-deep in debris, waving her arms and talking to the tall, white-haired man with the captain's bars on his shoulders. She was saying, "Captain Houlihan, she came in on the first bounce!"

Captain Houlihan turned to Sergeant O'Shaughnessy. He said, "Make a note of that, O'Shaughnessy. First bounce."

O'Shaughnessy made a note of that.

Bessie Barnum said, "All right, Captain Houlihan, speak up! What happens now?"

Captain Houlihan said, "Well, Bessie, we got her dead to rights. Flying a bathtub without a license."

Sergeant O'Shaughnessy shook his head emphatically. He said, "No way, Captain! We can't lay a glove on this lady!"

Bessie Barnum let out a Cherokee war whoop. She said, "Whaddaya mean we can't lay a glove on this lady? Jesus Christ, she's out roaring around town in George Washington's goddam bathtub and you stand there and say we can't lay a glove on this half-cracked old pelican?"

Sergeant O'Shaughnessy said, "Captain, she's the one I was telling you about! This broad's got a big clout with the Pope!" He bowed his head, closed his eyes and made the sign of the cross.

So did Captain Houlihan.

Just before Barb dropped me off I told her what the Johnny Huskin Evangelistic Association account was worth and she nearly lost control of her powder-blue Mercedes-Benz.

59

The morning was hot and so was my office. The *Chicago Globe* had made quite an issue of the Red Sea Documents. The precious papers had fallen from the skies "like manna from Heaven" and the religious implications had been duly noted. There was no mention of William Tell's bow and arrows or of Elizabeth Fudge and her marvelous flying bathtub.

The Sherwood Forest Pub opened at ten and I was there at 10:05. Mary O'Rourke brought me a Stroh's and a manila envelope. She said, "This is the July stuff on that evangelistic association account and Bertha will have the August report next week. She was in yesterday after work and Kenny Blossom made a pass at her."

I said, "Kenny Blossom wouldn't know what to do with her if she was standing on her head with an orchid in her snatch." I opened the envelope. Huskin was okay but there'd be no harm in looking. In July there'd been nearly half-a-million dollars deposited in the account but the balance was down to less than twenty-four thousand. Another big check to Children's Charities of Northern Borneo and numerous others to charitable organizations, local, national and international.

And one made out to Michael South.

And another to the Kenneth W. Blossom Detective Agency. My head was spinning.

I pushed the information back to Mary and said, "Thanks. Seen Mucho Macho around today?"

"I don't think he'll be in. Yesterday he said something about maybe having a business appointment at home." The little radio

MONASTERY NIGHTMARE

on the backbar cut loose with Willie Nelson singing "Blue Eyes Crying in the Rain" and I headed for the door. Mary said, "Luke, stick around! I'll turn him off!"

I said, "See you later."

I bailed my car out of the Adams Street parking lot and drove south to attend to some long overdue business. Then I stopped for a few beers and football conversation with Pete Nickeas at Dinkerty's Mill. Pete couldn't understand why the Chicago Bears were going to lose ten games next season and because such things require long and detailed explanation I didn't get back to my office until after two o'clock. The phone rang at 2:50. It was Jake Perry. He said, "Luke, you know where Kenny Blossom lives?"

I said, "Yeah, I've been there. Vicinity of Roosevelt Road and Austin. That's south of the Ike. Next door to a foundry. He's in the phone book, Jake. Kenneth W. Blossom."

"Can you get here in a hurry?"

"Depends on where you are. New Zealand's out."

"I'm at Blossom's house."

"Well, arrest the sonofabitch for mooching beers."

"Little late for that."

"Something wrong?"

"No, everything's just fine. Blossom's dead."

177

60

*K*enny Blossom, swashbuckling, tattooed, pink-shirted, six-gun packing, woman-ogling private detective, rented a run-down four-room house a few blocks east of Austin Avenue just south of the Eisenhower Expressway. The neighborhood was rough—blacks, Latinos, a smattering of whites, broken beer bottles in the streets, junk automobiles at the curbs, lopsided houses, banging, clanging factories, fly-infested delicatessens and lunch rooms, sleazy taverns with boarded windows and a clapped-up hooker on every third barstool. I'd been there, but only during daylight hours. Wild horses couldn't have dragged me into the area after nightfall.

The house was a soot-blackened, single-story structure and Kenny's flop-fendered, rusty, red Olds 98 was parked in the driveway ahead of a black, two-door Ford sedan. The Ford was a Chicago Homicide vehicle. There was a gathering of fifteen or twenty people clustered on the sidewalk and a blue-and-white Chicago squad car stood in front of the place, rack-lights flashing silently. I parked the Caprice and went up the steps to the sagging porch. The front door was open and I walked in. There were three men in the room, Jake Perry, a heavyset plainclothesman and a uniformed cop, all seated on a dilapidated sofa. Jake Perry didn't bother getting up. He thumbed me into a bedroom, hitchhiker style.

I'd seen happier sights. Kenny Blossom lay sprawled on his back across his unmade bed, his mouth agape and his watery-blue eyes fixed on the ceiling. There was a small, dark hole in the left front of his pink, imitation-pearl-snapped shirt and it was

MONASTERY NIGHTMARE

surrounded by a splotch of crustily dried blood. Under him a filthy sheet was stained claret. His shoulder holster was slung empty over the back of a wooden chair near the doorway. I left the bedroom and took a seat in a downright dangerous-looking rocker in the living room. Jake Perry hit me for a cigarette. He said, "Sorry to mess up your afternoon, Luke. What do you think?"

"I think you're right. He's dead."

"You saw Blossom a lot at the Sherwood."

"Not if I could help it."

"What I mean is you knew him, sort of."

"I tried to hold it at that. 'Sort of' was plenty."

"Who'd want to kill him?"

"That's simple. Everybody."

"I know that but what could he have been mixed up in that would get him blown away?"

"Anything that would turn a fast buck. Blossom wasn't particular."

The plainclothesman said, "Syndicate job, maybe. Blossom could have known something he wasn't supposed to know. I've seen him around and he talked a lot."

I said, "That doesn't cover it. The word is *incessantly*."

Jake Perry said, "Did he ever mention anything to you, anything out of the ordinary?"

"No. Some time back he said that he was on to something that would pay big money if he played it right but that was the story of Blossom's life. Anybody around here see or hear anything?"

"Not that we can turn up. Any goddam thing goes in this neighborhood and with that foundry thumping away next door nobody would have heard a bomb go off." Jake shook his head. He said, "Well, he had to be making a buck somewhere."

I said, "Oh, he picked up a job now and then. Divorce stuff, usually. How did you get hold of this?"

"Anonymous phone call. Would Blossom have gone as far as blackmail?"

"Only if he had someone to blackmail. He used to shake down the hookers at convention hotels. How long's he been dead?"

"The coroner will be here shortly. What kind of artillery did he carry in that showboat shoulder holster?"

179

Ross H. Spencer

"Pearl-handled .44 Colt six-gun. He made sure that everybody saw it. Where is it?"

"Gone. It's probably the murder weapon. Could Blossom have been involved with a broad?"

"He'd have liked that but I doubt it. In the first place he'd have told the world about her. In the second he was nuts about women but the feeling wasn't mutual. Why?"

Jake smothered a yawn. "Nothing important. We found a red rose on the bedroom floor. Odd thing to accompany a murder. Well, that's all, Luke. Thanks for your time. I owe you a beer."

"Sorry I couldn't have been of some help."

On my way out I passed a guy from the coroner's office and the meat-wagon was rolling up when I climbed into my car.

61

I called Crystal from a candy store on the south side. I said, "I just found some licorice and I'll be home in an hour."

"Itchy called this morning and I told him."

"You told him what?"

"That I'm pregnant."

I didn't say anything.

Crystal said, "He was very excited."

I said, "Not half as excited as I am." I jammed the bag of licorice into my jacket pocket and left the candy store. Too damn late. A black Cadillac was double-parked beside my car. Two lean, dark men got out. They were nattily dressed, blue suits, one with a gray vest, the other with a cream-colored turtleneck sweater. They met me on the sidewalk. Gray-vest said, "Inna car."

I said, "Whatta car?"

Turtleneck said, "Blacka Caddy."

I said, "Oh, thatta car."

Gray-vest said, "*Now.*"

In thatta car I said, "What's up?"

Turtleneck said, "Take you getta measured."

I said, "For what? Cement shoes?"

Gray-vest said, "White suit."

I said, "But I don't want a white suit."

Turtleneck said, "Sure, you want white suit."

Gray-vest said, "For First Communion."

62

*I*t was the next morning and Jake Perry was in my office, studying me coldly. He hadn't so much as mentioned the elevator. He was saying, "One of her studs found her this morning. He had a key. Did you have a key?" My stomach was churning. I shook my head. Jake said, "Did you know her well?"

"I worked for her."

"Uh-huh. Doing what?"

"Looking for her husband. What brought you to me?"

"Your name in her address book. In red, yet. She was one of the two clients in the Garvey matter?"

"Yeah."

"When did you see her last?"

"The morning after she introduced me to Jonas Solomon."

"The *morning* after?"

"About eight-thirty."

"You get around. Heard from her since then?"

"No. When did this happen?"

"Coroner's office said around three this morning. Thirty-two caliber. Silencer, probably. Nobody heard a thing."

Hillary Condor had used a .32 with a silencer and in *Murder Wears a Lace Brassiere* he'd shot both ears off a Filipino murder cult leader with it. At seventy-five yards.

Jake said, "What kind of gun you got?"

"Same one I had on the force. Thirty-eight police special. Licensed but I never carry it. Did ballistics check the slug?"

"Slugs. Four of 'em. Yeah, same gun that stopped Solomon. Where were you at three this morning?"

MONASTERY NIGHTMARE

"Aw, come on, Jake."

"I have to know, Luke."

"Home in bed, for Christ's sake."

"Alone?"

"Jesus!"

"Let's have it."

"No, not alone."

"Why, *certainly* not! Heaven forbid! Who was the broad?"

"She's not a broad."

"All right, who was the *lady*?"

"Crystal Ball."

"No time for comedy, Luke."

"All right, make that Crystal Balzino. She shortened it."

"Itchy Balzino's kid? That cute little blonde tyke?"

"Yeah, we're roommates."

Jake Perry closed his eyes and ran a slow hand across his forehead. "Good *God*, Luke, you just don't *give* a damn, do you?"

"Itchy's all right. He just wants me to turn Catholic."

"Damned small price for staying alive! Itchy worships that girl!"

"Makes two of us."

"You're really gone on her?"

I shrugged. "Jake, it just happened, that's all."

"Your business, Luke. Jennifer Garvey gave you no hint of trouble on her scene?"

"None. She was simply trying to ascertain if her husband's alive or dead. Right now I'm wondering about that myself."

"Why?"

"When she was married Jennifer Garvey did some swinging down the lane."

"Who told you this?"

"She did."

"Frank broad."

"Very."

"Well, she certainly wasn't swinging with that fruit lawyer of Garvey's."

"Hardly."

"Who's your other client, Luke?"

183

ROSS H. SPENCER

"Empire State Casualty Insurance. I got the job through Buck Westerville."

"That shit-heel on Wacker Drive?"

"Yeah. He's sort of a broker. He gets the jobs and passes 'em out. He makes a hundred a day on me."

"Westerville's a snake in the weeds. He'll get your ass in trouble."

"Not my ass. Somebody else's maybe but not mine. This is a kosher deal. Empire State isn't sure about Carl Garvey."

"And neither are you. You think he might be alive and killing people for past offenses, his wife because she skated around on him. Why would he hit the lawyer?"

"Possibly because Solomon handled affairs just a bit too cleverly."

Jake Perry found my cigarette pack on the desk and fired up. He said, "Not bad, Luke. Anybody ever tell you that you should get into writing?"

63

*I*t had taken a half hour to persuade Crystal to put on her clothes and go to the store. That accomplished, I'd said, "Buy something unusual, like meat and bread, for, lo, it is written 'Man shall not live by licorice alone.'"

Now I pushed the vestibule release button and listened to him climb the stairs. Heavy, slow footsteps, those of a man mounting the gallows. He walked into the apartment, head down, barely glancing in my direction. In the forty-some hours since I'd left him he seemed to have aged half as many years. He sank onto my couch and sat for a few moments before turning to face me with misery etched on his face. He said, "Awright, Lassiter, git on with it."

I sat beside him and lit a cigarette. I said, "I didn't want to go into it on the phone but the police found a murdered man yesterday. They also found a red rose on the floor of the room in which he was shot."

Huskin's voice was dull. He said, "Wall, Lassiter, I reckon y'all better do what y'all got to do."

I said, "I don't have to do anything, Reverend. I'm a three-for-a-dime private detective. I'm neither cop nor judge."

He sat, looking at the floor. "Y'all ever kill a man, Lassiter?"

"Yes. I was a Green Beret."

"How many y'all kill?"

"Three and a half."

"How'd y'all ever manage to kill half a man?"

"It took two of us to handle the fourth."

"Y'all feel real good about killin' these fokes?"

ROSS H. SPENCER

I shrugged. "Well, I haven't lost any sleep over it. It was a matter of staying alive."

Huskin nodded. "Yes, there is times when it boils down to that, one way or the other."

I took a deep breath and said, "Reverend, you picked the wrong gumshoe."

"I ain't never give you no complaints."

"Forget about me. I'm talking about the creep you hired to tail me when you asked me to follow your wife. What did Kenny Blossom have to report?"

"Nothin', Lassiter. He gave y'all a real clean bill of health. 'Course Blossom was th' kind of varmint who'd lay back an' play both ends agin th' middle."

"If you suspected me why the hell did you hire me?"

"I wanted to meet y'all so's I could see what kind of feller I might be up agin. I doan mind tellin' you that you come across purty fav'rable even if you was drunk."

"What made you suspicious of me? You didn't know me from the corner mailbox."

"Wall, Lassiter, lak I done tole you, Barb been actin' mighty strange of late. Thass how come I went over to th' telephone comp'ny an' requested a one-month transcript of all th' calls what got made from my home phone. One number kept croppin' up so I give it to this guy I heard tell of an' he tracked it an' it turned out to belong to Lassiter Private Investigations."

"You're talking about Mickey South?"

"Thass th' man. Runnin' down phone numbers is a sideline with him."

"Did your wife explain these calls?"

"I ain't never mentioned 'em to her."

I said, "Reverend, Mrs. Huskin's writing club wanted to invite a private detective to a meeting for a question-and-answer session. Call it research. Finding an available detective became your wife's assignment and she picked me out of the telephone book. She contacted me several times. I was dead set against it but she kept after me until I knuckled under."

"Y'all done met her then?"

"Certainly. I met her at a Blotters Club meeting. She's a

MONASTERY NIGHTMARE

beautiful, sensitive and highly intelligent lady. You're a very fortunate man."

"Why is it y'all never tole me 'bout this?"

"Because I don't maintain a private investigations business on the strength of violating the confidences of my clients. Let's get back to the nitty-gritty. Mickey South's specialty is telephone numbers. Blossom's was blackmail."

"I knows that now. Lettin' Blossom into my life was lak lettin' a coyote into a melon patch."

"I'm unfamiliar with the details. Fill me in."

Huskin looked away from me, directing his gaze to the blank screen of my television set. Very slowly he said, "Lassiter, Blossom was fixin' to blackmail me on account of I been layin' up with a woman."

"Candy Stoneman. At the Jack Rabbit Motel on Mannheim Road."

"How'd y'all know it was Candy?"

"She doesn't attend the club meetings at your house. You're never there either. I've met Stoneman. She has that easy look."

"How'd y'all find out what motel?"

"I had the phone number and Mickey South checked it out for me."

"But how'd y'all git th' number?"

"Kenny Blossom was responsible for that, in a roundabout way."

Huskin said, "Uh-huh." He lapsed into silence. After a while he said, "Back late lass fall Candy Stoneman showed up fer a Blotters Club meetin' at my house an' thass where I run into her. Next mornin' she called me at th' office an' said as how she wanted to write a book 'bout a preacher an' that she needed information 'bout religious beliefs an' things lak that."

"You volunteered your services?"

"I ain't sure. Seems like she kind of volunteered 'em fer me. Anyway, I met her fer lunch an' it turned out she was in need of a lot more than information 'bout religious beliefs. All this here happened at a time when Barb an' me wasn't winnin' on Nobel Peace Prizes an' I ended up in bed with Candy Stoneman afore I knowed whether I was afoot or on horseback."

"And Blossom tumbled to it."

187

ROSS H. SPENCER

"Wall, this here Blossom was a real bad feller but he wasn't no dumbbell. He knowed 'bout people. Soon's I hired him he tole me as how infidelity is usually a two-way street an' if one is out carryin' on, chances is th' other one's doin' th' same thing. Reckon I was thinkin' along them very same lines when I called Blossom. I was suspicious of Barb juss because of what I was doin'. It was my own conscience backfirin', y'see."

"How often did you meet with Candy Stoneman?"

"Juss 'bout ever' time they was a meetin' at my place."

"When was your most recent contact?"

"'Bout a half hour after you left White Birch Knolls th' other ev'nin'. Only reason I went was to tell her it was all over. Reckon I should of done it on th' phone 'cause Blossom was waitin' fer me. Tagged me straight to th' Jack Rabbit Motel."

"When did he lay it on you?"

"Yesterday mornin'. Called me at th' office an' give me his home address. Tole me iffen I had any serious intentions of keepin' on preachin' th' gospel we better git together fer a pow-wow." Huskin hauled out a handkerchief and wiped perspiration from his face. He was under extreme pressure. There are times when a man who's appeared before thousands will have difficulty with an audience of one. "I knowed ezzackly what he was up to 'cause he good as tole me on th' phone. Kept callin' me 'Reverend Jack Rabbit.' Wall, I druv out there li'l 'fore noon an' I reckon I done lost my temper. I went fer him an' he pulled a gun an' I grabbed it an' we went 'roun' an' 'roun' an' th' confounded thing went off an' next thing I knowed Blossom was stretched out on th' bed deader'n a doornail."

I said, "What kind of gun was it, Reverend?"

"Man, I didn't take time to look. I took it with me an' chucked it in th' Chicago River."

"Have you talked to anyone else on this?"

"Ain't nobody else I *kin* talk to 'ceptin' th' police when they shows up. Lordy, Lassiter, I wisht y'all knowed how to pray 'cause iffen y'all knowed how we'd git right at it."

I couldn't suppress my smile. I put my hand on Johnny Huskin's shoulder and shook him gently. I said, "Reverend, if we get around to praying the first thing we should do is ask God to forgive you for coming up here with an outrageous pack of lies.

MONASTERY NIGHTMARE

At first glance a gun collector of your enthusiasm would have recognized the make and caliber of Blossom's gun and he certainly wouldn't have missed its pearl handles. Nobody in his right mind throws his trademark, a red rose, on the floor of a murder room and blurts out a detailed confession before he's accused of something. You haven't killed anybody, accidentally or on purpose. You bluster around, threatening to shoot people, interlopers for example, and that's probably great stuff for household propaganda purposes but you aren't up to killing. If you could kill you'd have shot somebody long before now. Blossom's in hell but you didn't send him. You'd have given the bastard what he wanted and you'd still be paying him when that Millennium of yours gets here. Reverend, the fact of the matter is this—Blossom was dead when you arrived on the scene."

Huskin said nothing and silence grew heavy in the room. The big man sat, elbows on his knees, looking into space.

I said, "Kenny Blossom was an obscenity in the eyes of God and man. The world's better off without the sonofabitch. Now I'd advise you to forget about this entire affair and go home and shut up. Under no conditions should you discuss the matter with Mrs. Huskin because you won't have the remotest goddam idea what the hell you're talking about. Just take my word for it, everything's going to be perfectly okay and you and I are as square as we're ever going to be."

Huskin shook his head. He said, "Lassiter, was all them there Green Berets juss lak you?"

I said, "Yes, I think so. We lost the war in Vietnam."

He got up from the couch. On his way to the door he paused to glance at the old recording on my turntable, dusty and unplayed since July. He said, " 'Street of Dreams.' Feller doan hardly never hear that one no more."

I said, "No, it's an oldie."

"Y'know, Lassiter, thass my wife's fav'rite song. Funny thing, lass time I heard it was that there night y'all was trailin' Barbara. When y'all called me it was comin' over th' telephone loud an' clear."

I said, "Probably the radio in that service station I called from."

We looked at each other and neither blinked. Huskin's smile

189

was a weary, faded thing, a smile from a trash can in the alley of reality. He said, "Yeah, prob'ly." We shook hands and he went out.

I never saw him again.

Not even on television.

64

I went to the telephone and dialed. I said, "Your old man will be home in a few minutes."

"I suppose so. Then he'll go out back and sit on a hollow log. He's been doing a lot of that recently. I think he has something on his mind."

"I'm sure of it."

"Luke, I'm going to leave God's right-hand man. I've *had* it up to my *titties!*"

"No, Barb, you'll like Tennessee. They have stars bigger than baseballs down there."

She laughed. "You know where you can stick those stars bigger than baseballs."

"You're going to Tennessee, sweetie."

"The hell I'm going to Tennessee!" A kinky little frown had crept into her voice. "What's the matter with you?"

"Barb, you're headed south. You killed a man night before last."

"*What?* Luke, have you gone insane? Who am I supposed to have killed?"

"A man named Kenny Blossom. I've told you about Kenny Blossom and I've told you that he had an office on South State Street. When I mentioned that he knew the Red Sea Documents were missing you did some thinking. You realized that if he knew about the documents he probably knew about you and me. You called his office, recognized his voice and you'd found your blackmailer. You weren't bumming around before we went to the museum the other night. You'd made

191

ROSS H. SPENCER

arrangements to go to Blossom's home. You let him paw you until you could grab his gun and put him away."

"How would I know the man even had a gun? I'd commit murder to keep from getting cut out of a lousy thirty-some thousand dollars? Luke, in six months I can make more than that peddling my fanny!"

"Up until you took me home you were operating on the assumption that there was over a million bucks in that evangelistic association account and you were determined to protect your shot at it."

"I don't know what the hell you're talking about and I'm going to hang up on you!"

"You aren't going to hang up on *any*body but I'll tell you what you *are* going to do. You're going to button your lip to everybody about anything having to do with this mess. You're going to Tennessee with the finest man who ever came down the pike, a man who'd go to hell to protect you. You're going to settle down in a little white house behind a little white church. You're going to get religion and you're going to speak in tongues and believe in the Millennium and if you *don't* get religion you're damn well going to *pretend* you've got it. You're going to have a couple of nice babies and you're going to come home with your panties on right. You're going to walk the straight-and-narrow and be a good wife to Reverend Johnny Huskin for so long as ye both shall live."

"Or *what*, God damn you!"

"Or I'm going to build an airtight murder case against you and I'm going to make it stick. I'll hang your beautiful ass higher than a goddam kite! There ain't no seven-year statute where murder's concerned, kiddo!"

"My God, Luke, you've been setting me up for this and now it's *you* who's blackmailing me!"

"So long, Mrs. Huskin." I hung up. I got a can of Stroh's from the refrigerator, lit a cigarette and sat there in the late afternoon, hating myself.

Crystal came in, two large grocery bags rustling. She

MONASTERY NIGHTMARE

marched into the kitchen and in a moment she was back, slipping into my lap, naked as a jaybird again. I threw my arms around her and squeezed until she said, "Ooo-oof!"

I said, "Got any licorice?"

65

I called Buck Westerville from my office. I said, "How's *Monastery Nightmare* moving?"

"Last I heard they were considering another printing."

"So they've sold that first half-million."

"Apparently."

"Then, according to my figures, I've got about two hundred grand coming on hard-bounds alone."

"Approximately."

"And I've heard that the movie rights may go for more than a million."

"Possibility."

"And there's still foreign and paperback to be considered."

"Right."

"Then it's not inconceivable that I'll come out of this with something like four hundred thousand."

"I'd say it's almost a certainty. In due time, that is. What are you leading up to, Luke?"

"I have a deal for you, Buck. I'll take two hundred grand and walk. You and your people keep the rest."

"That wouldn't be wise, Luke."

"I didn't say it would be wise. I said I'd do it."

Buck said, "Well, you see, Luke, we couldn't come up with that much right now. The royalty period ends in December and Wellington requires an additional ninety days to compute and pay. The movie deal is still up in the air and so are the foreign rights and paperbacks. Actually all we've seen is that twenty-grand advance and you've received your share of that."

MONASTERY NIGHTMARE

"Buck, this whole goddam thing looks shaky to me. People are getting killed and I want out."

"Don't be that way, Luke! Solomon was queer and some rejected pansy did him in. Garvey's wife was shacking with the world and she got hooked up with the wrong tomcat. There's no connection between these murders and our thing."

"I'll bet you a truckload of Stroh's that Carl Garvey is alive and on a murder spree."

"Not a chance!"

"Buck, I've talked to Mrs. Garvey and to Solomon. I've talked to Pamela Frost. I've got a feeling about this."

Silence. Plenty of it. Then Buck said, "Luke, I've told you to stay out of the dark corners. You're going to hurt us if you keep talking to people you shouldn't be talking to."

I dropped it on him. I said, "Do you remember the name of the nuclear physicist in *Monastery Nightmare?*"

"Sure. Professor James."

"Do you have a copy of the book?"

"Of course."

"How about a Bible?"

"Yeah, I got one around here someplace."

"King James version?"

"Yeah, King James version." He chuckled. "I never turned Catholic. What's this all about, Luke?"

"Get your Bible and turn to the Epistle of James. You're going to decode the Professor James nuclear formula."

"All those goofy numbers? Do they mean something?"

"You're damned right they mean something. It's all in Chapter One of James. The first number gives you the verse, the second gives you the word in the verse and the third indicates the letter in the word. Call me back at your convenience." I hung up.

In less than an hour my phone rang. It was Buck Westerville, his voice an octave higher than usual, his words tumbling over one another like kids going to recess. "Luke, Jesus Christ, Luke, who else knows about this?"

"Nobody. *Yet.*"

"Luke, don't blow this thing for us! Give me a week and you'll

195

ROSS H. SPENCER

get your two hundred grand! Just a week, good buddy! Will you do that?"

I said, "One week, Buck, that's all. I'm going to the Fiji Islands and the hell with this entire fucked-up affair."

"All right, all right, I'll take care of it! By the way, Empire State Casualty just called. The Garvey investigation's been terminated and you're off the case effective immediately."

"Damned near."

"Damned near, my ass! Get off it and stay off it! You hear me, you rotten sonofabitch?" He was hollering now.

I said, "My, my, such language. The Catholics wouldn't touch you with a ten-foot pole."

66

A full moon floated like an orange beach ball on a torrent of frothing black clouds. A cool wind knifed from the west and a feeling of foreboding rode its current like a great, soft-winged ebony bird. Shortly after midnight I picked up Army Trail Road out of Addison, Illinois. I drove into the wind, watching my rearview mirror for the headlights of uninvited company. By the time I reached Route 59 there was nothing but darkness behind me. I eased through the tiny town of Wayne and in the distance I caught flashes of lightning. If this was a wild-goose chase it wouldn't be my first but it would certainly be my last. Within a few weeks I'd be with Crystal strolling the white sand beaches of Suva Point and letting the rest of the world go by.

Ten minutes west of Wayne I killed my lights and let the Caprice drift to a quiet halt a hundred feet short of the stone wall surrounding Carl Garvey's crumbling monastery. I took my flashlight from the glove compartment and my bolt-cutters from the trunk. I eased the trunk lid shut with a barely audible click. It was 12:39 A.M. and I watched the moon fall prey to an evil-looking pack of galloping dark clouds. Now there wasn't a star in the sky and the wind was cooler, almost cold. I reached the concrete pillars. I set the bolt-cutters and bore down on the handles. The chain gave way almost silently and young Lochinvar was within the gates. I walked up the long, curving, weedy drive toward the monastery, my feet crunching the gravel with a din that shattered the Fox silence. I stepped from the drive into the dry leaves blanketing the grounds and that was even worse. I might as well have brought along the Hubbard, Ohio, Drum and Bugle Corps.

This was a night to be ridden by the Devil and all the demons he could muster. The monastery's pin oaks swayed and groaned in the wind that was rapidly gaining velocity. Behind me the gates creaked and croaked on rusty hinges and leaves spurted from the floor of the property to fall and scurry erratically like terror-stricken mice. A fine place to make love, Pamela Frost had told me. Maybe so, but at that moment I could have thought of better. I approached the monastery warily, the way a sapper approaches an unexploded mine. It was larger than I'd thought it to be, approximating the size of a dairy barn, a collapsing two-story structure, obviously jerry-built, one that had required as many years in construction as in deterioration. It had been smothered under a blanket of spongy moss, and ivy tentacles swarmed up its sides like hydra, swaying, rustling harshly. Even the chill wind failed to carry away the unmistakable odor of decay.

I circled the old building slowly, my flashlight probing the darkness for an entrance. My nerves were on screeching edge when I came to a door set in the south wall. I discarded my bolt-cutters, twisted the door handle and pushed. The door swung inward without protest. I poured the beam of my flashlight down a long, narrow, cobwebbed interior. A huge rat interrupted the shaft of light for the space of the single heartbeat I lost at his unexpected appearance. Then there was a cataclysmic crash of thunder and the rain hit. It came in sudden, snarling fury, an insane flood of hissing water that flailed the area like a great cat-o'-nine-tails. Instinctively I fled from it, ducking into the hallway and feeling an arm encircle my neck.

I'd been keyed to the breaking point and I went off like a seventeen-dollar firecracker. I dropped my flashlight and drove my elbow into somebody's ribs. That broke the stranglehold and I spun to knee my assailant in the groin. When he doubled up I busted him in the back of the neck with everything I had. He hit the stone floor of the passageway like a bag of wet sugar. I retrieved my flashlight and rolled him over. He was a medium-built, bushy-faced character, well into his fifties, dressed in dark jacket and pants. I frisked him. He had no weapons. He stirred

MONASTERY NIGHTMARE

and sat up, staring with stricken eyes. He gasped, "All right, Garvey, you win. Get that light out of my face."

I said, "I'm not Garvey. Who the hell are *you*?"

He struggled to his knees, clutching at his crotch. He gritted, "Joe Cash, Empire State Casualty Insurance investigator."

"I'll be damned! Joe Cash, meet Luke Lassiter, also looking for Carl Garvey." I helped him to his feet and said, "Look, honest to God, I'm terribly sorry about this! Want a beer?"

"Damn right."

"Where's your car?"

"Out in the trees. There's a back way into this corner of Hell."

"Get your car and come around to the road. You can follow me."

Cash said, "I'm too goddam old for this roughhouse stuff. Where you headed, Lassiter?"

"Joint called The Embers up on Lake Street, late license place. Know your way around?"

"Hell, no. Took me a week just to find this monastery." He started for the door. He said, "One damn week too soon."

199

67

We were soaked to our skins. My shoes squished water and Joe Cash looked like a drowned spaniel. We sat at the end of the bar in the Embers, nursing bottles of Stroh's, kept company by a drowsy bartender, a fuzzy television picture and the roar of rain sweeping the roof. Joe Cash rubbed the back of his neck and smiled ruefully. He said, "I shouldn't have grabbed you like that. I was dead certain you were Garvey. He'd be quite a catch."

I said, "Forget it. I was wound so tight I'd have decked my own mother."

"Christ, that's a spooky old crypt. Chock-full of rats. I hate rats."

"Did you go through it?"

"Every goddam rotten inch. Take my word for it, Carl Garvey's not holed up in that place. Why, a guy could go off his rocker in there!"

"Think Garvey's alive?"

"For about ten seconds I did." He shook his head. He said, "But not before and not now. Garvey's gone."

"I've got a hunch he isn't."

"It's that screwy book. Somebody else wrote the damn thing."

"You're sure of that?"

"Why, sure I'm sure. Hell, Garvey never would have let Hillary Condor marry that slut Miriam Mission. Condor was too damn good for her!"

I grinned. "You a Garvey reader, too?"

"Yeah, since Condor's first case. Well, they got their publicity

MONASTERY NIGHTMARE

and it's working. The moving picture rights went for a million and a half a week ago. Invincible Films."

"Where'd you hear that?"

"The home office told me. Empire's really interested in Garvey."

"So am I. People connected with him are turning up at the morgue."

Joe Cash said, "Uh-huh, a gay shyster and a woman who'd spent most of her life looking at ceilings. I fail to see a devastating loss."

I said, "What's your next move, Cash?"

He snorted. "Back to the Big Apple, baby. A guy could get killed in this crazy town."

We finished our beer and I walked with Cash to his car. The rain had stopped and the skies were clearing. We shook hands and Cash said, "Well, so long, partner, no hard feelings." He smiled whimsically. "If you run into Garvey give him my best."

"I'll do that."

He climbed into his dark-blue Buick Regal and pulled into the night. I watched his taillights fade to the east on Lake Street. He'd go back to New York, I'd go to Suva Point, we'd never see each other again and it wouldn't matter at all.

201

68

I pulled in at the Rusty Pump on Mannheim Road and grinned off a few pointed comments on my disheveled appearance. I payed Slick the barkeep the thirty-five dollars I owed him, drank a brace of beers and drove slowly homeward through nearly silent streets still glistening from the heavy rain. Well, the party was just about over and I wondered if they sold licorice in Suva. The Morris Hedstrom store by the bridge would be the best bet. I was beginning to like the stuff. Like Crystal, it had grown on me. The good life was just ahead, the rainy afternoons for my typewriter and me, the nights on the beach with Crystal beside driftwood fires under stars set like frosty gems in skies of black velvet. I turned the last corner to find my block choked by vehicles with flashing lights. I pulled up three doors south of my building and got out of the car. A burly cop stabbed me with the beam of a flashlight and said, "Back it up, buddy! Emergency vehicle coming out!"

"What's the trouble?"

"Woman shot. Move your car!"

"Who? Why?"

"How should I know? They found her in the hall. She opened her door and got shot. Move that automobile, dammit!"

"What building?"

"That white-brick two-flat. Now do you move your goddam car or do you go to jail?"

I pushed the cop from my path and sprinted north. I vaulted the barberry hedge along the walk as the paramedics came out with the stretcher. I yelled, "Crystal!"

202

Monastery Nightmare

Her face was gray, her big dark-amber eyes foggy and less than half-open. I went to my knees and took her hand. Through dry, pale lips she said, "Good night, sweet prince." She shuddered and her hand went limp in mine. The big paramedic at the rear of the stretcher shook his head. He said, "Jesus Christ, how I hate this fucking job!"

I watched the stretcher go into the white van and a single word kept running across the blurred screen of my mind. *Sēläh . . . sēläh . . . sēläh . . .*

When I was a kid I'd had a puppy, a frolicsome thing with soft brown eyes. It had died and I'd cried the same way then.

69

Jake Perry sat in my platform rocker, long legs crossed, a small leather-bound notebook on his knee. He said, "Luke, I'd hate to be the sonofabitch who did this. He's one dead bastard."

"He is if I find him."

Jake frowned. "Leave it alone. He belongs to Balzino. Balzino will hang him by the scrotum over a slow fire."

"I got the matches."

"Any ideas, Luke?"

"No. I'm numb. Why would anybody hurt Crystal?"

"What did she know?"

"About what?"

"Any damn thing."

"Jake, Crystal didn't have enough sense to come in out of the rain. She was just . . . Crystal."

"For the record, where were you when this happened?"

"Probably at Fullerton and Mannheim. The Rusty Pump."

"Who did you talk to there?"

"The bartender. Slick."

"Slick?"

"Frank Harder. They call him Slick."

Jake was making notes with a steady scrawl. "Prior to the Rusty Pump?"

"The Embers out on Lake Street north of Bartlett. Drinking beer with a guy named Joe Cash."

"Who's Joe Cash?"

"Insurance investigator out of New York. Snoops for Empire State Casualty. We're looking into the same matter."

204

MONASTERY NIGHTMARE

"Carl Garvey?"

"Carl Garvey." My voice sounded hollow and a million light-years away.

"Where can I get in touch with Cash?"

"I haven't the foggiest. He was through in Chicago. He said he was going back to New York."

Jake stood up. "Mind if I make a couple of calls? Local stuff." "Phone's in the bedroom."

I could hear Jake talking in there, keeping his voice down. I sat looking at the picture of Carl Garvey on the back of the *Monastery Nightmare* dust jacket. Reality hadn't hit me yet but I knew it was out there, waiting in ambush.

Jake returned and eased his lanky body into the platform rocker and I said, "Now what?"

"Just waiting for a call from downtown, Luke. Shouldn't be long. Okay?"

"Yeah, sure." We sat there, exchanging glances, saying nothing, Jake Perry leafing through his notebook and smoking one of my cigarettes from the pack on the coffee table. I concentrated on Carl Garvey's dust jacket photograph.

Jake closed his notebook and slipped it into his jacket pocket. He said, "Luke, sometimes don't you wish you were a kid again?"

I said, "I've been a kid since a night back in July. Now, my God, I feel so old."

The phone rang and Jake got up to amble into the bedroom. I took *Monastery Nightmare* and a ballpoint pen from the coffee table. I sketched a bushy growth of hair onto the features of Carl Garvey and felt a chill flicker up my spine.

Jake came back and this time he didn't sit down. He stood in the middle of my living room, watching me intently. He said, "You're okay, Luke. The bartender at the Rusty Pump goes along."

"Thanks, Jake. I'm tired. Does that do it?"

"For now." He went to the door and opened it. He said, "Oh, by the way, Empire State Casualty has never heard of an investigator named Joe Cash."

I said, "I know, Jake. I just figured that out."

205

70

I buried myself in my apartment. No newspapers, no radio, no television, nothing. The phone rang a few times but I ignored it. At one time or another every man jack of us walks the Valley of Despair and I spent two days and two nights in that long, dark, rocky sonofabitch—bleak, blank desolate hours, haunted by the smiling ghost of a naked, jutting-breasted, slim-hipped, long-legged nymph with huge, dark-amber eyes and a lamebrained way that had completely captivated me. She'd loved me, God knows why, with a right-down-to-the-ground sort of love that a man can seek forever and never find. I sat on the edge of my bed, mopping my burning eyes and fondling the cold blue steel of the .38 police special I'd taken from my bottom dresser drawer.

Carl Garvey or Buck Westerville? Carl Garvey had motives for killing just about everybody in sight and Buck Westerville owed me a ton of money that he had no intentions of paying. I'd spooked Buck with the solution to the Professor James nuclear formula code and, for all Buck knew, Crystal could have been hep to the key. Either of us could have blown his jackpot scheme into the next hemisphere.

One or both, I didn't give a damn. If somebody didn't get to me first I'd balance the scales. There was nothing left. Crystal was gone, Suva Point had died with her and that was fitting enough. They'd become synonymous in my mind. Well, what the hell, nothing lasts forever. I'd climb out of this quagmire and splinters would fly.

MONASTERY NIGHTMARE

I laid the .38 on the nightstand atop Crystal's big book of Shakespeare and I rolled into bed.

Tomorrow or the next day or the day after that. Sooner or later. Tremble, thou wretch, that hast within thee undivulged crimes, unwhipp'd of justice. Shakespeare.

I'd looked that one up all by myself.

71

*T*he morning was gray. There was a penetrating drizzle. Graveside attendance was small. A withered little Italian priest spoke briefly. It was over in a hurry and Itchy Balzino turned away, wiping bloodshot eyes, Gray-vest and Turtleneck walking behind him. I met them at their black Cadillac. I put my hand out to Itchy. He took it and his voice cracked. "Hey, kid, is now all over. Tears no help."

I said, "I've done my crying. Let's talk."

Itchy turned to Gray-vest and Turtleneck. He said, "Go get drink. Come back in hour."

They trudged away in the rain, disconsolately obedient, and Itchy and I climbed into the backseat of the Caddy. I said, "There's a man I want to see."

"Is free country. Go see man."

"Can't. His office is locked and his phone doesn't answer."

"Who's guy?"

"Buck Westerville, the missing persons man. Can you help?"

Itchy Balzino scratched the back of his neck. He shook his head sadly. He said, "Not now."

"Why not? You know him."

"Buck Westaville somewhere else."

"Where is the bastard?"

"Funeral parlor, Elston and Lawrence. Pemberton's. Is nice place."

"Who died?"

"Buck Westaville."

"He's *dead*?"

MONASTERY NIGHTMARE

"Better be. Already embalmed."

"What happened?"

"Bullet."

"Who?"

Itchy shrugged and scratched a hairy ear.

I said, "One more." I took out my doctored photograph of Garvey and handed it to Itchy. He looked at it impassively. He said, "Who this?"

I said, "A guy named Carl Garvey."

"Garvey fall off boat and drown."

"No, he's still alive. I've met him."

"When?"

"Three nights ago."

Itchy scratched his shoulder. "They find boat on lake. Is empty."

"That was last October."

Itchy shook his head. "Seven o'clock lasta night. You ought watch ten o'clock news sometime. Even get baseball scores." We listened to the rain on the roof of the Cadillac. "Hey, kid, what you do now, no more Crystal?" His chain-saw voice was almost gentle.

I said, "I wish to God I knew."

He thumped the bulge of my shoulder holster with gnarled, knowing knuckles. "Put away cannon. Do like Crystal tell me. Go somewhere, write book. Leave killing to professionals." He winked at me and a tear rolled down his scarred cheek. "Write nice book about Crystal. She's be proud." He buried his head in his waffle-iron hands and sobbed.

I got out and walked to the Caprice. The rain was heavier now. I slammed my car door, lit a cigarette and sat there for an hour of that dismal morning, surrounded by tombstones, missing Crystal Ball like I'd never missed anyone in my life.

It wasn't over yet. One clay pigeon remained.

I started the car and eased out of the cemetery. I drove north and stopped at a drugstore.

I called Pamela Frost.

209

72

In mid afternoon I clomped wearily up the stairs of the Peerless Building. Homicide's Lieutenant Jake Perry sat dozing on the top step of the third-floor landing. He gave me a jaundiced look. "All right, Luke, what about it?"

I shrugged. "I don't know, Jake. Maybe they'll *never* fix the damn thing."

"Forget about the elevator. Where've you been?" He got up and followed me into my office to sit on my couch while I shuffled through my mail.

I said, "Oh, hither, thither and yon. Laid low for a couple of days, attended a funeral, talked to a guy, had lunch with a lady, drank some beer, thought things over and here I am."

"Luke, just what is it with you?"

"I'm not following you."

"Well, *don't*! You get within ten feet of somebody and here comes the hearse. You talk to a lawyer and he winds up dead. You work for a woman and she's gone in practically no time. You do a little drinking with a private shamus and he's murdered. You live with a girl and she gets killed. You do odd jobs for a missing persons guy and they'll bury him tomorrow. Always the same gun, except in Blossom's case. There comes a goddam time when coincidences ain't coincidences anymore. Luke, what the hell are you involved in?"

I frowned and shook my head.

Jake said, "It's getting monotonous. We got five stiffs and you've been connected with all of 'em in one fashion or another."

MONASTERY NIGHTMARE

"Make that six. Crystal was pregnant."

"Sorry, Luke. Then, to frost the cake, Carl Garvey's boat does an encore and they find it again, out on Lake Michigan again, *empty* again. So it could be seven. Of course you know nothing about the Westerville thing."

"Can't help you. Buck had sleazy connections and he may have crossed a line."

"Somebody's running a Class A vendetta and I think you know who. Is it Itchy Balzino?"

"He wouldn't shoot his own daughter. Use your head."

"Maybe that was an accident. Maybe you were the target."

"Maybe somebody wanted *both* of us."

"I've thought of that."

"I've thought of it since Crystal was killed. Jake, I'm blowing this shooting gallery."

"When and where?"

"As soon as I can scrounge up a passport and get properly inoculated. There's a freighter leaving Frisco for Suva, Fiji, in a week."

"That'll be expensive."

"Itchy Balzino gave me one helluva six-horse parlay."

"Going alone?"

"No, I'm taking a memory."

"Damn fool question. You'll *have* to go alone. Everybody you know is *dead*."

"Not quite. There's still you and Mary O'Rourke and there's old Nick Spanzetti at the newsstand."

"Scratch Nick Spanzetti. He dropped dead of a heart attack Sunday."

"I didn't know he had a heart condition."

"He *didn't* until the Cubs swept that doubleheader. Coming back?"

"Someday, maybe."

"Well, look, Luke, don't be in any great rush. If you come up a little short I'll pass the hat down at Homicide. The boys at the coroner's office ought to be good for a bundle." Jake got up and we shook hands. He said, "Hate to see you go but just now it's

211

ROSS H. SPENCER

probably for the best. If you hang around long enough you're a cinch to get hauled in as a material witness." He grinned. "Are you sure that Fiji's ready for you?"

I said, "I think they got some kind of militia."

73

At Bessie Barnum's Circus Tap I shook hands with Stash Dubinski. He said, "Call me when you get back to town."

I said, "I won't have to call you. I'll just drop in at Bessie's."

Stash said, "Luke, it's been fun."

I whacked him on the shoulder, went out to my car and drove southeast. It was nearly midnight when I locked the Caprice and trudged up the back steps to Mary O'Rourke's kitchen door. I rang the bell and in a few moments the kitchen light went on, then the porch light. The frilly curtains at the window parted briefly and the door swung open. She was wearing a brown chenille robe and, if I knew Mary, not another stitch. Her hair was up in blue plastic curlers and she was barefooted. She grabbed the cuff of my sleeve the way a terrier grabs a bone. She tugged me into the kitchen, rubbing sleep from her eyes. She said, "Hi, stranger."

I said, "Mary, I've been all tied up."

"You look tired."

"I am."

"Then come to bed."

"In a few minutes. Got a beer?"

"Sure thing." She popped the top on a can of Stroh's, turned off the overhead light and switched on a small lamp. We sat at the kitchen table and Mary said, "I heard about Mucho Macho." She held a match for my Marlboro. "Damn small loss but it still came as a shock. What was it all about?"

"Blackmail."

"Who did it?"

"I know at least two people who had good reasons."

ROSS H. SPENCER

"He was blackmailing them?"

"He was trying."

"Well, *tell* me, dammit!"

"Married couple, both of them cheating. Blossom picked up the trail and he was taking a whack at milking them separately."

"They didn't know about each other?"

"He knew about her affair but she didn't know about his. He found Blossom dead, figured that his wife had done the job and tried to take the rap for her."

"Oh, Luke, that's simply *beautiful!*"

"Yeah, ain't it? Right out of a 1935 Grade B flick."

"Did you know these people well?"

"Well enough."

"Was he acquainted with his wife's lover?"

"Yes, they were friends, I think."

"Oooo-o, sticky! Not *now*, I'll bet."

"Yes, even now. It's hard to explain."

"Well, I'd think so. Does this man's wife know that he knows?"

"Doubtful."

"Does he know that his wife's lover knows that he knows?"

"I'm certain he does."

"So who killed Mucho Macho?"

I sighed. "Mary, if it's all the same to you I'd just as soon drop the subject."

"It depresses you?"

"Yes."

"Me too."

I extinguished my cigarette and glanced up to find Mary studying me. She said, "Luke, you're sick and tired of it all."

"Yeah."

She left her chair and pulled me to my feet. "Let's talk about it in bed."

We talked about it in bed.

214

74

*T*he *Pancho Reyes* was an oil burner, a Liberty ship launched in mid-'44, a rusty, banged-up old bucket, fatigued but seaworthy enough to bum around the Pacific hauling anything from copra to reconditioned farm machinery. Our room was small but it was clean and comfortable. There were two other passengers, a gushy, white-haired old lady with a toy black poodle named Ferdinand and a man I hadn't seen. He took his meals in his room and he stayed there. When you're seasick, you're *sick*. For several days the Pacific had been like blue glass but just south of the equator the creaking, weary tub began to plow turbulent water and there were sharp gusts of wind. We were in for something. It was shortly after eleven at night when Pamela Frost said, "Luke, let's go up on deck."

I said, "I don't recommend it. There's a storm brewing."

"I know, and I've never experienced a tropical storm."

"There are better pastimes."

"Are they scary?"

"They'll do."

She gave me her toothy smile, picked up her big handbag, groped for her thick, white cane and said, "Wonderful! Shall we go?"

She gasped at the strength of the wind and I squeezed her heavy arm reassuringly. She said, "Oh, Luke, isn't this exciting!" She was like a kid at a county fair, all chirpy and bubbly. Since leaving Frisco she'd simmered down in bed. Not that she wasn't active but she'd stopped busting up the furniture and I'd lost most of my intimidated feeling. The night was pitch-black and

Ross H. Spencer

the decks were deserted. I guided her to our regular spot, a secluded nook above the old freighter's screw where we were screened by several lashed-down wooden crates stamped PIMSTONE, QUEEN'S ROAD. She placed her handbag at her feet, leaned on the rail and breathed the moist night air. She said, "Tell me how it is out here!"

"Well, the water is the color of licorice." I nearly choked on the word.

"Keep talking! Describe it for me!"

"It's like looking out over a boundless, black, boiling desert."

"Excellent alliteration! Oh, you'll be a writer, all right, Luke Lassiter! Go on!"

"There are no stars, no moon, the darkness is nearly tangible and visibility is rotten."

"I'm accustomed to that, Luke."

"Sorry. I shouldn't have mentioned visibility."

"No offense. Gosh, the up-and-down motion of the ship is so pronounced! Why, it's like being on a giant teeter-totter!" She grasped my arm and giggled. "Would it be a good night for a murder?"

"Ideal."

"Light me a cigarette, Luke, and let me enjoy this!" I got my old Zippo percolating, lit a Marlboro and handed it to her. This was to be the night, sure as hell. She said, "You haven't mentioned your story. I hope you're sketching it in your mind."

"All the time."

"Good! Is it a Casey Carruthers story?"

"No."

"Awww-w-w, Luke! But it *is* a mystery?"

"Not anymore."

"Well, *tell* me about it! Take it from the very beginning."

I took a deep breath. Here went the old ball game. I said, "Well, there's this literary agent."

"Male or female?"

"Female, more or less. Calculating sort."

"What's her name?"

"Let's try Pamela."

"I don't know that I like that, Luke."

216

MONASTERY NIGHTMARE

"You shouldn't. Pamela kills people. She'll book passage for two clear to the Fiji Islands in order to set up a murder."

I watched her beefy hands tighten perceptibly on the stern railing. She said, "Really, Luke? And who does Pamela kill?" Her voice was calm and lightly sarcastic.

I said, "Oh, Pamela isn't particular. She kills attorneys, loose ladies, pregnant women, hustlers, writers, anybody who stands in her way."

"Pamela does these things?" Her tone was mocking as she reached for her oversized handbag on the deck.

I said, "Don't waste your time. It's in there but it isn't loaded."

"What are you talking about?"

"I'm talking about a Smith & Wesson .32 with a silencer."

For so heavy a woman she was quick. Her thick, white cane came around in a sizzling blur. I lunged inside its arc and ripped it from her hands. I tossed it overboard. She said, "What are you doing, you fool? I'm *blind!*"

I plucked her large smoked glasses from her nose and dropped them into the inky Pacific Ocean. I looked into her perfectly focused strange gray eyes. I said, "Yeah, you're blind! You're about as blind as a goddam eagle but I have to say one thing for you! You really have that blind stare down pat!"

Pamela Frost said, "You're mad!" Her voice was sibilant, like the hiss of a cornered diamondback rattler.

I said, "Let's talk about how it worked. Years ago, when you sold 'Lilacs Are Fatal' for me, you spotted me as a potential replacement for Carl Garvey. When you found use for me you tried to locate me but I'd changed addresses half a dozen times. This sent you to a missing persons man on Wacker Drive. Buck Westerville had known me for years, he was a fox and he sensed that you had something cooking. He was the right guy, a larcenous sonofabitch, and you two hit it off famously. By the time the dust had settled Buck had dealt himself in and he helped you put your package together."

"Oh, this is utter nonsense, Luke! Fiction of the worst possible type! Pure tripe!"

"Hear me out, you'll like the plot, it's a dandy! Buck did your legwork and in return for promised shares of the action he

217

secured the silence and the full cooperation of the only two people likely to kick up a ruckus, Jonas Solomon and Jennifer Garvey. Then he conned me into writing a Garvey-style yarn and you submitted it to Wellington Books, representing it to be Garvey's final effort. Wellington jumped on it, it hit big and suddenly there was one helluva lot of money on the line, the biggest chunk of which was one and a half million dollars from Invincible Films. That payment came, of course, to the agent who'd submitted the manuscript, the same agent who'd submitted *all* of Garvey's stuff, the only person capable of bringing off such a hoax without leaving question marks all over the place— Pamela Frost of West Monroe Street. With that kind of money in your hand why hang around waiting for royalties and fringe sales? Eliminate your associates and *travel!*"

"Now, Luke, that's enough!"

"The hell it is! Pam, you picked people off like *rabbits*! As the brains of the scam you had easy access to your fellow conspirators and who'd ever suspect a woman who'd gone conveniently blind when she'd begun to hatch this thing? I suppose that most of us deserved to be murdered but not Carl Garvey and not Crystal. Jesus Christ, not *Crystal* just because she'd typed a manuscript! Crystal knew nothing. She honestly believed that I'd written the entire Hillary Condor series and that 'Carl Garvey' was my pen name!"

"Oh, Luke, for God's sake, stop and think! Carl was responsible for these deaths! Consider his motives!"

"I've done that. But it wasn't Carl Garvey. The man had blown his bonnet. He'd been driven to the wall by a slippery attorney and a promiscuous wife. His brains were scrambled and he was out in that old monastery licking his wounds. He knew he was being had, he knew who was having him and it was eating him up but Garvey's not a murderer. How did you kill the poor bastard and get his boat back onto Lake Michigan? The *Miss Fortune* was tied up at Burnham Harbor and that took some doing. Who helped you? What did it cost you?"

"Luke, so help me God, I haven't been near Carl Garvey since he disappeared the *first* time!" Pamela Frost was tough. I had her by the short hair but she wasn't throwing in the towel.

I said, "Knock it off! Garvey was fouling the gears. He knew

MONASTERY NIGHTMARE

too much. He spotted my car near the monastery. He got my license number and he probably slipped a St. Charles cop twenty bucks to trace it for him. He tailed me and he connected me with everyone in the group, Westerville, you, Jennifer and Solomon. When *Monastery Nightmare* was published he put the pieces together. Garvey had to go."

Pamela Frost stood clutching the rail, the wind ripping at her loose, graying-blonde hair. She extended a big hand to me and said, "Luke, we could have a wonderful life together. We'd have all the money we'd ever need and I'd develop you into a fine writer. I'd make it happen for you. Casey Carruthers would become a household hero!"

I said, "Oh, but you bastards were cute! I'd no sooner started to worry about my piece of the cake than here came Buck Westerville with all that mumbo-jumbo about looking for Garvey. After Buck it was Jennifer with the same routine. Then Jennifer gave me the old come-hither act and so did you and I was up to my stupid ears in red herring and getting well paid to stay that way." The main mast of the *Pancho Reyes* tilted spectacularly against the backdrop of ominous sky and the exhausted vessel screeched in metallic agony. I said, "When Buck told you about the solution to the Professor James nuclear formula code you knew that you had to clear the decks in a hurry and you nearly swung it. I'm the last of your Mohicans and *I* wouldn't be here if I'd been at home on the night you killed Crystal. Still, I wasn't positive until you invited me to lunch on the day of Crystal's funeral. Why would a blind woman pay to transport a busted-down relic to the tropics? So he can *write*? Huh-uh! You had to have a better reason than *that*, a reason like getting me alone at midnight on the deserted stern of a tramp steamer during a blow. I'd been thinking like a goddam ostrich, first assuming it was Westerville or Garvey, then figuring that Itchy Balzino had turned his boys loose on *both* of them just to make damn sure he got the guy who'd shot Crystal."

"Itchy Balzino? Are you talking about the underworld figure? What can he possibly have to do with this?"

"Buck Westerville never mentioned Itchy Balzino? Well, big mama, he *should* have because Balzino's the most powerful

219

hood north of Sicily and he's the father of the girl who lived with me!"

"Her name was Ball."

"Her name was Balzino until she shortened it."

"What does this gangster know?" There was no expression in her voice. It was flat. She sounded like a fourth-grader reciting "The Village Blacksmith."

I said, "He knows enough to make him mighty damned curious when he comes out of the shock of bereavement. But he won't be curious long. He'll get the entire story the very damn minute we tie up at Suva."

"My God, Luke, what are you going to do?"

I said, "Well, when we left Chicago I had every intention of killing you but I've changed my mind. Instead, I'm going down to our room and transfer half of that million bucks from your suitcase to mine. Then I'm going to stand clear and let you spend the short remainder of your life looking over your shoulder. This planet isn't big enough to hide you from Itchy Balzino. Sooner or later you're going to find yourself staring down the barrel of a pistol." I put my hand on her shoulder. I said, "Who can say, Pam? It may be a Smith & Wesson .32 with a silencer."

She nodded, a half-smile toying with the corners of her wide, thin-lipped mouth. She said, "Not a bad story after all, Luke. I'm sorry I criticized it earlier. Perhaps you should write it."

"Perhaps I will."

"A few words of advice before you begin. You're going to have to learn about subplots. The average short story can get by without a subplot and so can the type of action yarn written by Carl Garvey but a good novel requires one and I can help you in that regard."

"Don't bother."

Her half-smile was gone, replaced by one of full proportions. "Now, why don't we introduce another character into your novel, a private detective named—well, let's see, why don't we call him 'Kenny Blossom'?"

"What about this new character?"

"We could arrange for Kenny Blossom to be inordinately occupied with the comings and goings of Luke Lassiter. We could have him visit Lassiter's office one afternoon and notice a

MONASTERY NIGHTMARE

portion of a manuscript written by Lassiter, a manuscript entitled *Monastery Nightmare*. Do you like that?"

"Not particularly but continue, please."

"Let's suppose that Blossom's surveillance of Lassiter has served to uncover a link between Lassiter and Pamela. Blossom knows that Lassiter has been to Pamela's office, that he has taken Pamela to dinner and that he has spent a night with her. You might mention that Lassiter isn't quite up to Pamela's sexual requirements."

I said, "Pamela can't use a forty-year-old man. Pamela needs a young Brahma bull. Tell me, did you pose for Blossom's tattoo?"

She ignored it. She said, "It follows then that Blossom's curiosity is aroused when a best-selling novel named *Monastery Nightmare* comes out under the name of Carl Garvey, a writer once represented by Pamela, a writer who's been dead for nearly a year. Are you with me?"

"Not yet but I'm gaining."

"Kenny Blossom is a very cunning man. He's talkative and he's repulsive but he's terribly shrewd and he puts two and two together. He gets five instead of four but he's close enough. He thinks that Pamela is working hand in hand with Lassiter on a million-dollar hustle and he attempts to blackmail Pamela."

"Which is like trying to milk a cobra."

"Exactly. You're good with similes, Luke. He's also trying to blackmail Lassiter."

"Not a dime's worth."

"I don't believe that, but no matter. Pamela has no choice but to kill Blossom. Since feigning blindness she's kept an automobile in a northside garage. She drives to Blossom's residence and she arrives just in time to see Lassiter get out of an old Chevrolet Caprice. She slows to watch him enter Blossom's house, she parks and waits long enough to hear a single gunshot, muffled but still audible in spite of the foundry next door."

I stood mutely, waiting for the axe to fall. Pamela Frost's soaring laugh blended with the wind soughing in the sparse rigging of the *Pancho Reyes*. I'd misread this one from the outset. She was stark, staring insane. She said, "Pamela circles the block, returning to find Lassiter's car gone and Blossom's

221

door unlocked. She goes in and finds Blossom on his bed, shot through the heart and, gratifyingly, very, *very* dead." She watched me for a moment, her mad gray eyes glittering with triumph. "How's *that* for a portion of a highly intriguing sub-plot, my aspiring-writer friend?"

I shrugged. "Pamela has witnessed this?"

"With her very own eyes. Good, isn't it, Luke?"

I stifled a false yawn. "For a blind broad it's downright amazing." I turned and walked away from the fat, clever woman who'd traded her soul for a suitcase crammed with green paper.

Much as I'd traded mine to help the man I'd wronged.

The wind was howling now and it was beginning to rain.

75

I lay facedown on the bed, listening to the old ship creak and groan in the storm that had pounded us since I'd come below decks.

Pamela Frost had pulled an ugly black rabbit out of her hat and we had a Mexican standoff. She was a formidable opponent, this bulky, red-faced, masculine creature with the intellect of an Einstein and the instincts of a Centruroides scorpion.

She had me pinned to the wall. I'd killed Kenny Blossom because he'd deserved to die. He'd been a disease-carrying parasite with his mandibles plunged into the life stream of an almost thoroughly decent human being. I'd wiped out three and a half men in Vietnam and Blossom's human value hadn't raised my grand total to four. I'd shot him as I'd have shot a swamp adder.

I felt the *Pancho Reyes* swing sharply to port, pitching and yawing in the vast, churning chasms of a thoroughly enraged Pacific Ocean. I heard rapid footsteps in the passageway. They slowed, then stopped and there was an urgent pounding on the door. It wouldn't be Pamela Frost. She had a key. I left the bed and opened the door. The first mate of the *Pancho Reyes* stood in the hall. His name was Bob Krieter and he was an efficient, affable fellow from Franklin Park, Illinois. Water streamed from his long, yellow slicker and his eyes were wide. He hesitated before blurting it out. "Jesus, Mr. Lassiter, your lady friend's over the side and so's our other male passenger!"

I stared at Bob Krieter, unable to speak, feeling shock roll over my face.

Ross H. Spencer

Krieter said, "I was leaving the bridge and I saw you coming from the stern. Then, just a moment later, I saw him step out of the shadows."

I found my voice and said, "Who? *Who* stepped out of the shadows?"

"Our other male passenger, the guy who never left his room! Man, the way he embraced her I thought maybe they had something going on the side!"

"He *embraced* her?"

"Well, whatever it was, I mean he really *grabbed* her! Next damn thing I knew both of them were gone!"

I sprinted down the hall and headed topside, three steps at a time, Bob Kreiter right on my heels. The *Pancho Reyes* was running a tight circle, crashing through mountainous, frothing black waves, searchlights clawing futilely at the raging water. We struggled against a screaming wind to reach the railing and in a split second I was drenched. The suffering World War II antiquity was buried in an awesome avalanche of sound and Krieter yelled, "Not a chance, Mr. Lassiter, not in *this* sea!"

I shook my head. Gone, all of them but me. I was the last of a star-crossed cast. Crystal's beloved William Shakespeare couldn't have plotted it better, even at his gory best.

Bob Krieter grabbed my shoulder and steered me toward the companionway. I went down the steps dazedly. At my door Krieter said, "Miss Frost was a real nice lady but I hardly ever saw *him*."

I said, "Who the hell *was* he?"

Krieter squinted. He said, "Well, I never looked at his papers but he signed the manifest as Hillary Condor."

When twilight velvet drapes the island of Viti Levu, a stooped, white-haired American leaves the lounge of the Grand Pacific Hotel in Suva. He plods eastward, along the beach track, until he reaches a certain hollow log and here he sits to study the myriad wonders of the tropical night. When the Southern Cross has reached its zenith in that vast, star-strewn cathedral, when the night waters of the eternal Pacific have lulled the old man, he leaves the hollow log and crosses the narrow road to his cottage, very much alone save for his constant companion of many years—a sturdy, white, wooden cane, washed ashore by the tides of Suva Point.